LIMBS

A Love Story

TIM MEYER

Grindhouse Press
PO BOX 521
Dayton, Ohio 45401

Grindhouse Press #046
ISBN-10: 1-941918-44-1
ISBN-13: 978-1-941918-44-9

Also by Tim Meyer

NOVELS:

In the House of Mirrors
The Thin Veil
Less Than Human
Sharkwater Beach
Kill Hill Carnage
The Switch House

The *Demon Blood* series:
Enlightenment
Gateways
Defiance

The *SUNFALL* series (co-written with Chad Scanlon and Pete Draper):

SUNFALL: Season One
SUNFALL: Season Two
SUNFALL: Season Three

COLLECTIONS:

Worlds Between My Teeth
Black Star Constellations

For all the lovers out there.

acrotomophilia. a·crot·o·mo·phil·i·a. noun. The deriving of sexual gratification from fantasies or acts involving an amputee.

– *Yourdictionary.com*

ONE

"HI, my name is Ray, and I'm an amputee," I lied with a straight face, a lie I told so many times before. So many that I almost believed my own bullshit.

Almost.

I wasn't an amputee. Far from it, in fact. But they didn't know that. They never did. To them, I was Ray Bridges and I blew my arm off in a New Year's Eve fireworks accident. Told them I'd been drunk and lit a short fuse and didn't have the reaction time (because of the booze) to get away. Boom. Told them my arm had disappeared behind a fury of sparks and smoke, my flesh and bone splintering into fragments, an exploding *human* firework. Snapped my available fingers, told them my arm was gone just like that. Told them that was the last memory I had of two working arms.

Not really, though.

But that was what I told them, and like always, they bought the act. After all, they had no reason to question me. No able-bodied person would sneak into a support group meeting for amputees, most of which were usually held in hospital basements and local YMCAs. No able-bodied person would pretend to be an amputee just so they could sit next to a *real* amputee. To get closer to them. Start conversations with them.

Conversations that would eventually lead to sex.

Okay, let me stop there. I know what you're thinking. I know the types of thoughts circling the space between your ears, the kind of image you're projecting of me. I'm a monster, right? I'm some horrible human being who pretends to be disabled so I can weasel my way into the pants of amputees, especially once they've arrived at their lowest low. I'm talking new amputees. Fresh. Recently recovered from their surgeries and starting to experience the real world as an amputee for the first time. The people who wake up and for the first fifteen minutes of their day completely forget they're handicapped, that they've lost a vital piece of their existence.

Okay, I guess I can agree with you to some extent—a part of me *is* a monster. On the surface, this looks bad. I get it. I guess it's the treacherous nature of pretending. The trickery. The lies, the deceit. The fact there's a certain level of manipulation involved. I guess if you look at my situation on the surface and don't dig an inch deeper, I *am* a predator, someone who preys on the weak for personal gain. I hate that word—*predator*—but I'm trying to stay objective here, step outside my own head and see your point. These women who'd experienced something terrible and life-altering, who were at the lowest point of their existence, whose self-esteem had reached rock bottom—they were, if you want to be a dick about it, my prey.

But I *wasn't* a monster. Correction—I *am* not a monster. And I'm definitely not a predator, some sexual deviant prowling the streets—or, in this case, support group meetings—for an easy piece of ass. Okay, essentially that's what I was doing, but not really. I was—

Okay, look. Can I start over?

No? Fine. Look, here it is, plain and simple; for me, it was never about manipulation. It was never about the sex, per se. Sure, it was, to some degree, but also, it was something much more than that. It wasn't about using them, tricking them into believing me to be something I wasn't. It wasn't about luring them into the bedroom. It wasn't only about orgasms and filling some void within myself with hours upon hours of weird sex.

It was that I found them beautiful.

Yes, that's right. Their disfigurement. Their missing arms, legs, fingers, knees, and toes. Physically, I found them attractive.

There's a word for it. It's called acrotomophilia. Someone who is sexually aroused by the physical deformities of others—specifically, amputees.

I don't know how it all started. Not exactly. I guess it began during my childhood, right around puberty. Maybe I saw an amputee, a gorgeous blonde with one arm sitting in a restaurant or walking through the mall. Maybe I thought, *what if?* Maybe that idea, as strange as it sounded, followed me through that impressionable time of young adulthood when you form bonds with your body and mind, when you begin to discover yourself. Maybe I researched it on the Internet. Maybe I found out there were others like me, those who also wondered *what if?* Maybe I looked at amputee porn. Maybe I masturbated to it. Maybe from then on it was the only thing I found attractive, the only thing that kept my engine running. Maybe from then on, able-bodied women just didn't do it for me.

That's a lot of maybes. Not entirely sure I'm willing to discuss everything here in great detail, but that's close enough to the truth. You get the point. Bottom line: I was only sexually attracted to amputees, and I discovered that much about myself from a young age. They were the only ones that could turn me on. And I know what you're thinking, so I'll answer the question before you ask: yes, I had tried to ignore it, tried to have sex with someone who did have all their arms and legs, and no, it didn't work. I tried to pretend, close my eyes and envision them with a severed arm or an absent foot. Even asking them to hide one leg under the sheets didn't work. It was the knowing, I think. The knowledge it was there. Attached. Whole. Made me softer than your favorite pillow.

Okay, you might think I was sick. That I had a problem. That I should have sought help, maybe *see* someone. A professional. Someone who could help. Change me. Fix me. Make me . . . well, make me *not this way.*

But I would disagree. I didn't think I had a problem (still don't). I thought I had a preference. And besides the lying, the deceitful nature of certain tactics, what was wrong with it? I didn't think anything (still don't) but you're welcome to disagree. I was just a guy with a kink, I guess, and I would never apologize for it. These women who had gone through difficult times—I was there for them. I was there when no one else was.

Want to hear something crazy? 93% of amputees admit to being depressed post-incident. Over a quarter of them attempt suicide. The women I'd been with after they'd lost a piece of themselves? None of them had ever tried to kill themselves after being with me. Shit, most of them stopped going to meetings. They left me happy. Free. Untethered from the worries no one would want them. Show them affection. Love them.

I gave that to them. Freedom.

In a way, I'm kind of a hero.

Okay, that's a stretch. I realize that. But seriously, I'm not a monster.

At least, I wasn't back then.

TWO

SMOKE clouded the sky near the exit, and I walked out into the fog confidently, riding high from a pretty good meeting. My arm hurt a little, as it had been pinned tightly against my side like a human version of a chicken wing, but I ignored the pain—it was well worth it. I usually wore baggy clothes to hide my ruse, a sweatshirt several sizes too big, and that night was no different. Thank God it was winter and the comfy pullover worked as the perfect disguise.

I'd been going to these things for a little over a year now—not many of them, mind you—and not once had anyone called me out. It was a lot easier when I played the role of the able-bodied group leader, a volunteer position anyone with a background in psychology can be nominated for. Which I did have. Sort of. If you count the one class I took over at the community college a little over a decade ago and my short stint at a mental health facility when I was twenty-four.

I moved to the end of the walkway where the group of smokers congregated. Fixing my eyes on my mark, I asked her, "Can I bum a cig?"

She smiled faintly, her eyes narrowing against a cold gust of wind. I looked down at the name badge tacked above her left breast: WENDY, it read. Not that I didn't already know it. I had listened to her story. And it was a good one.

"Wendy," I said.

"Sure thing," she replied, her green eyes glistening in the bold moonlight. She was smiling, sure, but her eyes were hiding the despair. She was broken, I could tell. On the verge of losing it. One insult or one able-bodied person's disgusted glance away from having a complete mental breakdown.

She offered me the pick of the pack. I plucked one free and popped it into my mouth.

"Need a light?"

"Absolutely." With the only hand she had, she lighted my smoke.

I sucked in the cancerous cloud, ghosted breaths.

"Come to these often?" she asked, that certain twinkle catching her eye. I could tell she found me attractive. I felt the same way about her. She was a little older than me. Not old enough to be my mom, but we were definitely talking about the difference of a decade. Her face held a few wrinkles. Some extra meat clung to her bones, something that never mattered much to me. Her right arm was missing from the elbow down. Car accident. Two months earlier, she'd been driving and hanging her arm out the window. Some drunk asshole speeding down the opposite lane almost hit her head on, side-swiped her instead. She never saw it coming. She said she'd blinked and the next thing she knew her car was on the side of the road and her arm was gone, fountains of blood were gushing from where it had been connected.

"Yeah. Not this one, though. I'm visiting friends. Actually live about two hours that way." I pointed east with my cigarette. Most of that was true. I did live two hours east. I wasn't visiting friends, however. I had a rule–never attend a meeting in the same town where I live, or the same county for that matter. Nope, I would always travel. Hit different meetings in different towns. Never score in the same town twice. It kept me from getting caught. It was safer. Getting caught was not something I wanted hanging over my head. It was bad enough I felt a twinge of guilt for posing as an amputee for personal gain, but to be confronted about it would be the proverbial dagger in my heart. "How about you?"

She swallowed, her eyes unable to focus on mine. She wasn't comfortable talking about such things. Not yet. "Yeah . . . so . . . this is, um, actually my first meeting."

"Really?" I sounded genuinely surprised. "You sounded like a pro in there."

"Thank you." She giggled softly. "Thank you. This . . . this hasn't been easy on me."

"It's tough. I know." I wrapped my free arm around her, pulled her close. Rubbed her shoulder. "You'll get through it. We all will."

(I should stop and mention I've always felt terrible about this. That none of this ever made me feel good on the inside. There's a part of me that wished it could be different. That I could be honest. That I could tell her, *Hey look. I'm an able-bodied person and I find you very attractive and I want to take you home and bang your brains out.* But I'd actually tried that approach, many times, and . . . well, those instances didn't end very well. A story for another time, perhaps, but long-story-short–that specific angle had earned me a trip to the emergency room. Twice, actually.)

I let go of her. I didn't want to be too touchy-feely. That was just plain creepy. No one liked a creep. Even though my touch was probably soothing, comforting, gently refreshing–touch a stranger too long and you cross that invisible line of unpleasantness.

We smoked. The poison felt good in my lungs. I didn't smoke often, but when I did, it always calmed me down. Relaxed my nerves. I suppose that was the point. If it wasn't so goddamn unhealthy, I'd become a full-time smoker in a heartbeat.

We were almost out of tobacco. Most of the other attendees had left. Two ex-soldiers, both of whom were confined to wheelchairs after having their legs blown off by IEDs in Iraq, lingered near the outskirts of the parking lot, quietly talking about how long it would take to get their prosthetics. I got the sense they were only there because we were. A part of me thought they were watching me, waiting, seeing if I'd make an attempt to kidnap Wendy. Which was ridiculous, but I guess that's the age we live in. Everyone's on their toes at all times.

"Want to grab coffee?" I suggested.

"How's about something stronger?" she fired back, an almost

reactionary response. "A beer?"

I was a little taken aback. It wasn't usually this easy. But I saw the pain behind her eyes. There was something there, something she didn't share in the meeting. She was hurting for other reasons, something else besides being forced to live this life sans a limb.

Maybe someone left her after the accident. A husband, perhaps. I saw no ring and honestly, that situation was all too common. Spouses find it difficult to cope with the reality their partners will never be able to walk again. That they'll be a burden on them. The stress can be too much for some people. *Weak* people. A lot of them end up leaving. It's a sad fact, but it *is* a fact. Not everyone is fit for that life. Not everyone can cope. The world is filled with weak people, and it takes situations like these to highlight them.

By now, you may be thinking my little scheme was solely sexual. It wasn't. I mean, sometimes it was. Have you ever gone out to a bar or a club with the sole mission of getting laid? Of course you have. Men do this. Women do this. There's nothing wrong with it. We're all adults and we all have needs, desires we like to fulfill. But sex wasn't the only thing I was after on these escapades.

This was how I dated. Sort of. There were other ways. There are plenty of Internet sites dedicated to this sort of thing. I mean, of course there is. There's an Internet site for everything nowadays. But I hated them. There were some real weirdos on those sites, and you never knew what you'd end up with. No thanks. I would stick to this. Meeting people. *Real* people. Getting to *know* them in person, not through some digital universe of selective anonymity.

So there was the truth: I was thirty-two years old and I wanted to settle down with someone. Get married. Have kids. Live the American Dream, white picket fences and all.

So here I was.

About to have a beer with Wendy.

My arm had begun to hurt, but I didn't care. It was so worth it.

When we got back to her place, she shimmied out of her jacket. I helped her with my one available hand. I kept my sweatshirt on. As soon as I tossed her jacket on the couch, she was on me—kissing my mouth, drawing her hand down my chest, over my belt, caressing my swelling member. She stopped after she touched the bulge in my center pocket, realizing how turned on I was.

"Is this okay?" she asked playfully.

"Yes," I said, and kissed her back. Gently at first. But the next thing I knew, her arm was around my neck and she was pulling me into the bedroom.

I threw her on the bed. Unbuckling my pants, I let the denim fall to the floor. She was propped up on her elbow. She was smiling. Her legs were spread. I imagined her without pants on, knowing I wouldn't have to imagine much longer.

"Take your shirt off," she demanded.

This was always where things got tricky. *Always.* It was bound to happen. Naturally, sex often involves two naked parties. And, considering I didn't want to blow my cover, that couldn't exactly happen on my end. So, I used *the excuse.*

"Is it. . ." I hung my head. I hated acting. Pretending. This part hurt the most. The guilt of it all hit like a hammer in the center of my chest. ". . . is it okay if I leave it on?"

Her face traced shadows of concern. Opening her mouth, she chose not to answer.

"It's been a few months," I told her, "but I'm still . . ." My chin trembled. I brought forth tears, not heavy enough to fall. ". . . just not ready yet."

She sat up. Wrapping her arm around my neck again, she smooched my earlobe. "Of course, baby." Her voice was almost motherly, and strangely, that wasn't a turn-off. But I rotated into her face and kissed back.

"Thank you."

I looked at her stub and my blood pumped, furiously now.

We fell onto the mattress.

Outside, a wolf howled in the distance. Somewhere in the wild, a hunt began.

THREE

I rolled into work about fifteen minutes late, and Debra, the store greeter, smiled and welcomed me like any ordinary customer, even though we'd worked together for the last two years and have seen each other almost every goddamn day. I smiled back and played along, then asked her who the manager on duty was.

"It's Glen," she said in the same tone as if someone had unexpectedly passed away. "So, you know." She stretched her lips to the sides of her face, an exaggerated expression that said *watch-the-fuck-out-man.*

And I would steer clear as best I could. Glen was kind of a dick. Okay, maybe not *kind of.* He *was* a dick. Huge one. Monumental. I expected my lateness would earn me a write-up, but that was okay. I'd been working at Best Tronics for three years and I hadn't gotten a single late during my employment. I'd only called out twice. I had enough sick time built up I could have taken a month off, paid-leave. I planned on accruing two months and taking a vacation to Europe or something. I was thirty-two and had never been out of the country. Barely been out of New Jersey, now that I mention it. Sad, I know.

Before Debra could trap me in some banal conversation, I heard footsteps behind me. I turned, expecting to find Glen and his beady stare judging me and wondering if I was still drunk from the night before, but it wasn't Glen. It was my friend, my only *real* friend, Percy Jones.

"What's up, killer?" he said, punching me in the arm. It hurt more than I thought it should. His knuckle had connected with my bone. I thought about giving him a shot back, just to keep things even, but he'd hit *my* punching arm and I could barely lift it.

"Fuuuuuck, dude."

"Sorry." He rubbed his knuckles with his other hand. "Shit, I think that hurt me more than it hurt you." He nodded at me. "Glen's looking for you, man. Better hide in the back or something."

"Shit, already?"

"Yeah, man. He's a time clock hawk, you know that."

I shook my head. He'd write me up, for sure. "All right. Where is he? Office?"

"Where else?"

I started toward the back office.

"Where were you last night, anyway. I missed you. I got *Dude Bro Party Massacre III* on Blu-ray. Evan and I got Taco Bell, got really stoned, and we watched it twice."

"I had some things going on."

As mentioned, Percy was my best friend. Usually best friends tell each other everything. Right? That's how it works? But he didn't know about me and my monthly excursions around the state. He didn't know about the meetings. About my preference when it came to women, that the only way I could get off was with someone who'd lost a limb in some horrific, life-changing way. He didn't know *those* secrets. And he probably never would. Unless I found her. *The one.* A future wife. If I got married, he'd be my best man. Then I'd probably tell him.

In all the years I'd known him, he never once asked why dating wasn't all that important to me, why I never mentioned the women I'd been with. I had always assumed he thought we were alike—awkward and uncomfortable around women. Unable to attach to those of the opposite sex because we had come from fragmented families. Fatherless, with no real strong male role models. (I don't actually know if that's true or not, but some quack during my brief stint at the local mental health facility said such things, and at the time it had made a lot of sense.)

I don't know. Percy just never asked about it, pushed the issue, and I never volunteered the details, fearful if I had told a single soul, the information would get out and then my life would be ruined forever.

But would it?

I believed so.

"Okay, Mr. Secretive," he said, grinning almost knowingly.

He doesn't know shit.

"Oh, stop."

"Hey, man. You don't want to tell me, that's cool. As long as you're not a serial killer, that is. I mean, it'd be pretty cool, I guess, but also kind of fucked up."

Percy lived and breathed horror movies, especially those obscure, low-budget trash films the average person can't stomach, and not because of the content, the bloody carnage and high body counts, but because of the poor production quality. He'd been a film student at the local community college, and he shot a few short films locally. His dream had been to move to Hollywood and become the next John Carpenter. I supported him no matter how far-fetched his goals had sounded. I'd even helped him out on the shorts, standing in as an actor or an extra. I'd even once held the boom mic for an entire shoot. Whatever he needed, I was there for him.

Percy slapped me on the back. "Relax. I'm fucking with you."

"Yeah."

"You okay?"

I snapped out of my flashback of last night. My time with Wendy. It had been fun, but unfulfilling. The sex was average and lacked something basic, a fundamental connection nonexistent. No sparks. No romance. Nothing that made me want to stay for breakfast.

Anyway, at the very least, I hoped I'd given Wendy a confidence boost. If I ever saw her again, and I hopefully wouldn't, I hoped her eyes would look a little less sad. A little less void of despair.

"Yeah," I said.

"Yoooooouuuuu sure?"

Before I could provide a reasonable response, a group of new hires, fresh off their orientation, walked in a line right behind Percy. Leading the pack was my favorite manager, douche bag extraordinaire, Glen. He stopped when he saw us.

Saw *me.*

"Bridges, you're late," he said, his upper lip curling as if I disgusted him in some way. No *good morning,* no *how's it going?* Just, *you're late.*

I almost wanted to tell him to fuck his own weasel-y face. But I needed this job, so I held my tongue.

"Yeah, I'm really sorry, Glen."

He didn't address it any further. Instead, he turned to Percy. "All the DVDs and Blu-rays put away like I asked?"

Percy winked at him. "On it, boss." He immediately spun toward the aisles of movies, leaving for the work that should have been finished before the store opened.

Glen shook his head, clearly disappointed. He faced me again, forming that snooty pouting thing he did with his lips whenever someone didn't listen to him. For whatever reason, it ignited a rage within me. He was such a dick. I wanted to tell him that, that and to fuck his own face-hole. But again, I needed the job, the benefits and the competitive hourly rate, so my lips remained closed.

Maybe one day I'd have the courage to punch him.

"Bridges," he said. "Meet the new additions."

There were four of them. Odds were only one of them would last longer than a month. Most of them would work through the Christmas season, head back to college come February. The one survivor would work here until they found something better or they'd get stuck here until the corporate leeches sucked their souls dry, rendering them a lifeless minion of retail hell. I'd seen both happen all too frequently. Hell, the latter was happening to me right now. Every day I felt a little less like myself and more like an android with the Best Tronics logo stamped on my forehead.

"This is Felicia, Robbie, Trevor, and Kayla."

I said "hello" to all of them. I didn't plan on remembering their names. I never remembered names until they'd worked here for at least six months.

But Kayla stuck with me for some reason. Maybe it was the way she smiled at me. Maybe it was her hair, the faint pink streaks that complemented the bleached blonde. Maybe it was her body. No, it couldn't have been that. Too many limbs, too many arms and legs. Sometimes I hated my preference, my acrotomophilia. It made me feel abnormal, like something was wrong with *me*.

Kayla made me feel like I should be attracted to her. But I wasn't.

Simply too many arms and legs.

Too many fingers.

God, I was such a freak.

Percy popped his head around the corner. Looking over the newest MacBook model, he whispered, "New girl is pretty hot, huh?"

"Huh?" Somewhat startled, I jumped, just slightly, not enough for him to notice. More surprised about the nature of the topic than I was about Percy appearing unexpectedly. Him popping up in random places while on the clock (and supposed to be working) was actually quite normal. "Oh, yeah, dude. Really hot."

"You didn't ask which one?"

My eyes darted. "Which one of what now?"

"Dude, are you even paying attention to me?"

"Yeah, sorry. I was thinking."

"So which one?" His face slacked. "Dude."

"I don't know."

"Felicia or Kayla?"

I looked over at the newbies. They were over at the registers up front. Glen headed the gathering, instructing them how to greet and ring up customers according to corporate's SOP. He fixed his glasses every thirty seconds or so, a nervous tic the entire Best Tronic's roster had taken notice to over the years, poked fun at him for behind his back. Now and then, someone would poorly imitate him in the break room, and the impressionist featured the tic every time, made it a huge part of the show.

Tool, I thought, and not for the first time.

"Well?" asked Percy.

"I don't know, man. Kayla, I guess."

"How come you never talk about girls?"

Oh, God. Here it comes.

"You gay, bro?"

I glared at him, cocking my head to the side and folding my arms across my chest.

"It's totally cool if you are, man. I'm not here to judge. I just, you know, as your best friend and all, should know these things."

"I'm not gay."

"Okay, okay," he said, throwing his hands in the air. "Because if you are, I'm totally cool with that. My friend Cody, you know, the big dude who helped me film *The Body Breaker* last year, dude with the long hair and the muscles the size of Glen's massive cranium . . . totally gay. Big gay. Super-duper gay. Really, super–"

"I get it."

"Anyway, I went to the Pride parade with him last year and everything. Great dude. Could totally hook you up with him if–"

"Percy," I said calmly. "I'm not gay."

"Okay, okay," he said again, this time pumping his hands, telling me to slow down. "Just wanted to let you know there is nothing wrong with it if you are."

"I agree. There's nothing wrong with it. But that's not it."

"Then . . ." He swallowed as if the next question were forbidden. "Then what?"

I sighed. I wasn't prepared to have this conversation with him. Not here, at work. "I'm just . . . *particular,* I guess."

"Picky bastard, huh? Hm. I get it. I respect it. I guess. But damn, dude. Look at Kayla over there, just look at her."

I snuck a glance.

"She's hot."

Though I didn't wholeheartedly agree, I did see it. Sans an arm or a leg, she'd be my kind of girl.

My dream girl.

"Yeah," I said, "hot."

I went back to booting up the computer displays and Percy returned to packing out the new releases, and neither of us spoke more on the subject for the rest of the day.

FOUR

NEVER comfortable in crowded places, I always food-shopped late at night, and never *ever* on the weekends. However, only two weeks away from Christmas, the grocery store was a little more populated than usual, with people getting their hams and turkeys and dessert trays, preparing for the big family dinner. The kind of family dinner I wished I'd had growing up. Being raised by a single mother with no siblings and the closest family member 400 miles away, a big family gathering never happened.

Picking out vegetables, I reflected back on the day and how shitty it had been, how Glen was a complete tool-bag and how I hoped he had the day off tomorrow. My thoughts also fell back on Kayla, the new girl. She was cute, I had to admit, even if she did have a complete set of limbs. She seemed nice too, and I only judged that based off her smile, and we all know how deceiving a nice smile could be. But there was something else about her, her *aura* if you will. If you believe in such nonsense, and to a certain degree, I do. She had this *aura* about her. An unexplainable feeling crawled inside me whenever I'd looked at her.

I had to shut my thoughts off. They were getting too weird, too *real.* I suddenly realized I'd been holding a cucumber for almost thirty seconds, staring into a small tower of vegetables. I snapped myself out of it.

"Ray?" someone called from down the aisle.

Putting the vegetable back, I craned my neck.

And nearly fainted.

"Ray, is that you?"

My throat closed like an angry fist. I wanted to say something, anything, but I couldn't get the words out. I must have looked like a complete fool, standing there speechless, the dumbest look baked to my face.

"It's me," the woman said, almost cautiously, and I could tell by the sound of her voice I must have looked at her as if she were a ghost, something that shouldn't exist. "It's Wendy."

I threw the cucumber back on the pile and tucked my arm against my side, the one that had been missing the first time we met. I leaned against the racking, trying my best to use the structure to my advantage. I don't know how well it hid my arm, but, well . . . I guess not very well.

"Wendy?" I squeaked. "What a . . . what a *pleasant* surprise."

She pushed her cart beside mine and stretched out her arm, attempting to hug me. Awkwardly, I leaned forward, still keeping my arm pinned behind me. I threw my other arm around her and pulled back immediately.

"Good to see you again so soon," she said.

I guess I nailed the angle right because she didn't notice my arm. Maybe my position, how I leaned back from the hug, helped some.

"Yeah, yeah, you too." I scratched my chin. Every speck of my flesh suddenly felt itchy. "So, um, what are you doing here?" *Two hours east,* I almost added. This was not supposed to happen. This was why I drove two hours to hook up. For instances exactly like this.

"Oh, my mother lives in Galloway. I stopped here on the way to visit her. Gonna cook for her tomorrow."

"Oh, how lovely." I forced a smile and wondered if it came off genuine enough or not. Probably not. But this was my hell. This was my nightmare.

The encounter stumbled along nicely until a little old woman, who should have been in bed past eight on a Tuesday night and not up and about at the local food store, pulled her shopping cart up next to me and said, "Excuse me, sir, but can I get a cucumber?"

I almost told her *sure, take all the cucumbers you want. Just scram for five.* But I didn't. And I don't know why I didn't. Could be me Monday-morning-quarterbacking the situation, but that would have been the best move. Instead, I said, "Yeah, no problem," and proceeded to shift down a few steps, keeping my angle, my arm between me and the racking.

It had to be the most awkward movement ever.

Wendy fixed her gaze directly on me. Well, not *on* me. Around me. The thing dangling from my shoulder. My supposedly missing arm.

She eyed me, her suspicions raised.

"Well," I said, glancing down at a watch-less wrist. "It's getting late. They're closing soon. Better get all my stuff. Er, food."

Before I could wish her good night, she said, "It's a twenty-four-hour supermarket."

"Oh, is it? I wasn't aware."

"Hm."

That little vocalization sent an invisible stake through my heart. I'd been fucking caught.

"Why are you standing like that?"

"Like what?" I asked. My throat dried up like a desert on the hottest scorcher of the year.

"Like . . ." She pointed to my situation then twirled her finger as if that fucking explained everything. ". . . that."

"I, uh, I'm just . . . standing. Like normal."

"Turn around."

"Excuse me?"

"Turn around. Let me see you."

My eyes fell on the end of her jacket's sleeve, where a hand should have been, had that drunk driver never scraped against her. I felt crushed. Absolutely horrible. I know I'm not a monster—God, I swear I'm not—but in that moment, I sure felt like one. Worse than I'd ever felt since engaging in this dishonest business.

"Wendy, please, I can ex—"

She moved closer. Barely opening her mouth, she said, "Turn

around."

Pointing my chin toward the ceiling, I let out a desperate sigh. There was no use fighting it. She already knew. God, how the hell did this happen? I'd been so careful.

I showed her.

"You son of a bitch," she hissed.

"Wendy, I can explain."

"You . . . you tricked me."

"I didn't . . ." I immediately walked back that claim. "Okay, I did. Sort of. But—"

Pressing the heel of her palm against her forehead, she backed away. I wasn't sure what would happen next, but I prepared for everything. Everything from her passing out to her taking a few swings at me.

Instead of doing either one of those, her eyes turned on me. Her lower lip quivered. I could tell she wanted to explode. She wouldn't be wrong to.

"You . . . you took advantage of me."

"Yes," I said. There was no denying it. "Yes, but let me explain."

"Is that rape?"

"What? No. God, no. You were very into it."

"But I thought you were . . . you made me . . . it was under false pretenses. I thought you were like me, I thought you were an amputee. I thought we could . . . I dunno . . . help *heal* each other."

"I did a horrible thing, but I can explain. I'm a . . . God, this is so much harder in real life than it is in your head."

Her face wrinkled with confusion.

"Okay, look, I'm an acrotomophiliac."

"A crow-toe-what?"

"It means . . ." I looked around the immediate area. No one lingered around save for the elderly woman who seemed to grope each cucumber, seemingly enjoying herself way too much. I started to wonder if she intended to use them for cooking. "It means I'm only attracted to people with certain disfigurements. Specifically, in my case, amputees."

At first she didn't know what to say. Her brain processed this information, slowly, and she chewed on her tongue, tilting her head to the side. She opened her mouth to speak, but whatever words, whatever questions she had, never came forth.

"I know that sounds fucking weird. I barely understand it myself." Resorting to a good old-fashioned beg, I put my hands together in prayer. I'd never begged for anything in my life, and here I was, in the middle of the goddamn supermarket, begging. Hoping this woman wouldn't blow up my entire sex life. I didn't know how she could exactly ruin me, but with enough determination, I was certain she could figure something out. With enough determination, she could put an end to me. My life. My fraudulent ways.

I didn't think she had it in her, though.

At any rate, I hoped so.

No, prayed.

"What I did was terrible. I'm truly sorry. It's just . . . I find women like you . . . very, very attractive."

She averted her eyes, looking somewhat embarrassed. "So . . . you just go around using us? Is that it?"

"No. No, well . . . yes. I guess. But not really. Look. You're not just an object of sexual desire. If that's what you mean."

"I'm not?"

"No. You're a person. With feelings. And I take that into account."

"You take that into account?" That didn't sit too well with her. I wish I had something rehearsed, something I could spew out. Like a script. That was it—I should have had a script ready for just this scenario. Never thought this would happen in a million years. I was winging it and doing a terrible job.

"When I looked into your eyes the other night, I saw something."

Her stare came back to me.

"You were hurting. Fresh off surgery, right? A couple months? I listened to your story. A terrible thing happened to you. I felt . . . a connection to it." I touched my heart. The words weren't completely untrue, not all of it. I may have embellished certain things, but for the most part I spoke the truth. I did feel for her, felt for her in ways not too many human beings ever would.

I cared.

"So, what? You pity-fucked me?"

"No. What? Follow the conversation."

She bit her lower lip.

"Okay, I'm sorry. Here." I cracked my knuckles, realizing Wendy would never crack her own knuckles ever again. Not with her other hand. On her desk, sure. Maybe against her jaw. But not with her other hand, that finger-entwined stretch that was so goddamn satisfying. "My method was dishonest. I admit that. But the feelings, the connection, everything about that night was real."

She squinted as if my face would reveal a lie. Of course, it didn't. Because I wasn't lying.

"I know you were hurting. I thought . . . I dunno. Maybe someone left you. A husband or a long-time boyfriend." The sadness in her eyes grew. Expanded. Took over her entire face. "And I thought . . . maybe . . . here's a girl who could use some company. Some love. Even if it was for one night."

"You're such a martyr."

"It's true. I'm not making this up."

She studied me, a moment that—in my nervous frame of mind—lasted an eternity. Her harsh glare overstayed its welcome.

"Fine."

"Fine?"

"Yeah, fine. I believe you."

"You do?" Not what I had expected. I had fully prepared to ditch my groceries and run like hell. Out the door. All the way home.

"Yeah. I do. Should I not?"

"No, you should. I'm not lying. This is . . . this is the most honest I've been in a long time." That was the honest-to-God truth and . . . the truth actually felt kind of good. Maybe this was it. The kick in the crotch I needed. My wake-up call.

"Okay, good."

"Well . . . well, good then."

"But I won't forgive you. And I won't let it happen to anyone else."

My stomach dropped like a two-hundred-pound barbell. "What now?"

"If I ever see you anywhere near another meeting, I will call you out in front of everyone. Then I'll call the cops. Tell them . . . well,

I'll tell them something."

"Okay. Fine."

"I think you're sick and you need help."

"Wendy, I'm not sick–"

"Uh, uh, uh," she said, giving me her forefinger, shoving it inches from my face. "Don't *Wendy* me. You need to *see* someone. A fucking shrink or something. You're . . . you're fucking damaged, man."

I didn't want to point out the irony in that statement. But fuck, maybe she had a point. A small, minuscule, so-tiny-you-could-barely-see-it-with-a-microscope point. "So, just so I'm clear, you're not going to the cops?"

Took a second, like she mulled the option over again, but she finally said, "No. I'm not." Grabbing her cart, she squinted at me. Upturned her nose. "But don't give me another reason to. If I see you again. . ." She bared her teeth like a rabid raccoon and stormed off down the aisle.

I took a deep breath, collected my thoughts. The conversation had scrambled my brain. All sorts of thoughts came and went like cars at a busy intersection. Everything from "I need to quit this life-style" to "Maybe I do need to see someone" to "I'm fine" and "Where should I attend my next meeting and how far should I travel this time?"

My bladder had overfilled and I felt like I might burst from the waist down.

I turned back to my cart.

Next to me, the elderly woman measured the thickness of the cucumbers with a ruler she'd brought from home and licked her lips.

FIVE

AFTER I came, I rolled off Janet and rested my head on her spare pillow. Looking up at the ceiling fan, I caught my breath. She did the same, much louder than I. In my periphery, I saw her chest rising and falling rapidly. She wheezed. I sat up, staring at her collection of ceramic unicorns straight-on. They sat in a glass hutch, four shelves packed full, a shrine for the imaginary creature from her childhood dreams. Above it, she had tacked a poster of a unicorn drinking from a sparkling river in an all-encompassing greenish-blue aura, something that would engulf me if I dropped a tab of acid.

But I was sober and this was just . . . well, this was *Janet.*

"Was it good?" she asked.

"The sex?" I asked between labored breaths.

I felt her eyes on me. In her defense, I had asked a dumb question.

"Yes. The sex."

"It was great."

She struggled, but she raised herself to a sitting position. "Will you take me outside? I need a smoke."

"Yeah, sure."

I rolled off the bed, threw my clothes on, and made my way

around the room. Grabbing her wheelchair, I wondered how many more unicorn knick-knacks a person could have. The hutch had been stuffed to capacity. Her collection had started to spread to other areas of the room—her computer desk, her nightstand, and the shelves on the wall that used to display her favorite hardcovers. Now littered with unicorns of various shapes and sizes. In the three years I'd been "visiting" her, her collection had tripled.

I removed the rainbow-patterned unicorn hat, the one with a stuffed, half-limp horn jutting out from the top of it, from my head and tossed it on the desk. Then, I helped her into the wheelchair.

Janet had no feet. She didn't exactly take care of herself growing up. Overweight, she'd been diagnosed with diabetes at a young age. Despite pleas from doctors and family members, she'd refused to change her diet and lifestyle, and . . . well, she ended up having both feet amputated about five years ago.

She always claimed she'd change, switch up her diet from fast food to home-cooked veggies and lean meats, but I never saw any evidence to support her claims.

I wheeled her out the front door, onto the porch. Helped her light her cig. Took one for myself.

"You've been smoking a lot recently," she noted.

"Yeah. Well . . ." I shrugged. "Life."

"I don't think we should see each other anymore."

Those words stung. Like a whip cracking across my bare back. I froze up. The cigarette smoke bothered my eyes, so I turned away, stared out into the early-morning shadows. "Okay," I said. "May I ask why?"

"I don't think you really care about me."

The extra skin on her face jiggled as she spoke.

"Of course I do."

She shook her head. Tendrils of smoke climbed the air before her. "No. You just use me to get off."

It was true. Kind of. I used her the same way she used me. We were each other's crutches. That was the agreement we had. And she didn't know about my preference—not exactly. She might have suspected, but I never flat-out told her. Our relationship was purely sexual. Always had been.

"Janet," I said, slumping my shoulders. I bent on one knee to look her in the eye. "I thought we had an understanding."

"We did. But I don't want to anymore."

"All right." I sucked down the rest of the cigarette, not enjoying the burn in my lungs. "All right, if that's what you want."

"It is. I thought you liked me. Cared about me. But you don't. I can see it in your eyes."

"I do like you."

"Do you? You barely look at me when we fuck."

"I . . . huh?"

"Yeah," she said, hanging her head. "I know I'm not the most pleasant person to look at."

God, she was crying now. I checked my phone and the numbers read just past five in the morning. Luckily, I didn't see any neighbors readying for the early-morning commute.

"Janet, you're beautiful."

"Shut up. Don't pacify me."

"I'm not."

"I can tell, Raymond."

Shit, she called me Raymond. Only my mother ever called me Raymond when she was pissed. Coming off Janet's tongue, my full name drilled through my core.

"Okay, look. We have a thing going. A good thing. A not-so-complicated thing."

"That's a super shitty way of saying you're using me for sex and nothing else."

"I just thought we were helping each other out. That's all."

"And we were. But I don't want to anymore. I want to change myself. I want to lose weight. I want to be healthy. I want to stop collecting goofy unicorn shit like a fucking child. I want . . ." Her lips quivered. Tears spilled down her face. "I want a boyfriend."

"That's great!" I sounded generally excited for her. For the first time since I'd known her, she actually seemed interested in those things. This was a step in the right direction. I wanted to kiss her forehead, tell her how proud I was to hear these things. But instead I stood up and leaned against her porch railing. "That's really great, Jan."

She wiped her nose with her jacket's sleeve. Tears continued to fall, less steadily now. Black streaks of cheap mascara bled down the length of her cheeks. "I'm going to change. And that change starts with ditching you."

I flicked my cig into the bushes and headed for the steps. "I really hope it works out for you."

And I did hope that.

On the drive home, I tried to stay awake and thought about my life, how much *I needed to change.*

A few blinks later, I was home. Tired-drunk, I stumbled into my bedroom and flopped on the mattress, crashed asleep, and dreamed about Kayla.

We were naked. In bed. She had no arms. No legs. Nothing. Just a body and a head. Her limbs had been recently amputated; the stitches were still visible, holding her skin together in bunches. We were cuddling, post-fuck, nuzzling. Talking. Holding meaningless conversations. We laughed. We were happy. We shared kisses and stories. We shared love.

Then I woke. It was one in the afternoon.

I wasn't late for the closing shift. Could have been if I didn't hurry up, get my ass in gear and shower.

I dragged myself to the bathroom, in search of soap to scrub off Janet's smell from my body for the last time.

SIX

THE store was closing in fifteen minutes. I put away the returns, finished stocking the shelves, and I was about to hit the bathroom when Glen appeared (almost out of nowhere, I swear I don't know how he does it) in my path. He had that look about him, like he wanted something. His zig-zag of a mouth moved in preparation.

"Bridges," he said, bouncing on his heels. "You. Office. Now."

Fuck. He'd written me up for being late the other day. *I knew it.* I nodded at him, then followed his lead to the back.

As soon as I crossed the threshold of the manager's office, I saw her. She was sitting down in one of the three available seats. Glen took his seat behind the desk. Which left one seat open–next to *her.*

Kayla.

"Well, have a seat, Bridges," Glen said, motioning to the empty seat.

I quickly sat down. Nervously, I looked from Kayla (who smiled) back to Glen (who didn't).

"You're probably wondering why I brought you in here, Bridges. Kayla here finished her computer training a little while ago and it's time for her to hit the floor. Figured I could pair her up with you. You can show her around, show her what to do after we close. Stocking the shelves and putting away returns . . . you know, the usual duties."

I didn't tell him I'd already taken care of everything and planned on bouncing the fuck out of here at precisely closing time. That wouldn't have been the smartest move, and I'd already made some dumb decisions this week.

"Sure, no problem."

Glen smiled; this arrangement delighted him. This little talk may have been prompted by someone else—maybe Mark, the general manager. The man behind the curtain, so to speak. No one ever saw Mark. Ever. Some employees doubted he even existed. But that wasn't true. I'd met him before. He was like a puppeteer and a puppet never sees who pulls their strings. Mark pulled the Best Tronics' strings. Whenever Glen or the other managers ran around the store as if someone had set them on fire, we knew Mark had called the store. Or stopped by. Had a meeting. He was this omnipotent driving force, this legendary ruler.

Mark Barr—the God of Best Tronics Store #767.

"Good," Glen said, opening his hand, showing us the door. "Then go show her around. What are you still doing here?"

I turned toward her. "Ready?"

In her seat, she squirmed nervously. "Yeah. Definitely."

"Let's do it then."

"So, this is where the cashiers leave the returns," I told her, showing her the spot where the cashiers leave the returns.

She smiled. Her gaze shifted from the returns staging area over to the wall. Back again.

"You okay?" I asked, getting the sense her mind had drifted elsewhere.

"Yeah, fine."

"You sure?"

"Yeah," she said again, but I could tell otherwise. "Okay, it's just— I dunno, that guy Glen gives me the creeps."

"Manager Glen?" I asked, as if there were another Glen we'd come across in the last fifteen minutes. "He's weird, a huge dickhead, but he's relatively harmless. Just don't be late for work and do whatever he assigns you and he'll pretty much leave you alone."

She nodded, understanding.

"So, I usually separate the returns into four baskets," I told her. "One for each corner of the store. I take the—"

"So what do you do for fun around here?"

I froze, the question catching me off-guard. "Fun?"

"Yeah, so, like, my parents and I just moved to New Jersey. We lived in Buffalo, New York before that. Too much snow and my grandparents are getting older so we decided to move closer to them. I'll be honest . . . I've been here a week and I'm bored as shit. All my friends are in Buffalo and school won't start back up until the end of January, so . . . I guess, I need a friend."

She smiled and bounced on her toes. She seemed nervous, anxious—like her body was too small, too petite to handle all the energy bottled up inside her.

"Want to be my friend, Bridges?" she asked, calling me by my last name. Only Glen called me "Bridges", but coming from her lips . . . it sounded cool.

I allowed it.

"Uh, yeah. Of course."

"Good. Making friends is so hard when you're older. Used to be so easy when we were younger, in high school. Right?"

I snapped my fingers and pointed at her, an Elvis-esque move I'd never done in my entire life, but the situation had me flustered, not thinking clearly, and I was crushing on this girl fucking hard. "How old are you exactly?"

"Twenty-five."

I nodded.

"I know," she said, rolling her eyes. "I know what you're going to say. You probably want to know why I'm a twenty-five-year-old college student. Right?"

"No." I shook my head. "No, not at all. I'm thirty-two and I've been thinking about going back, actually." Shrugging, I told her, "It's no big deal."

"Yeah, well. I had a lot of . . . um, issues."

Issues were good. I had issues. Maybe she had some extraordinary kink, too. Like, guys who had an extra toe or something. Or weird growths under their arms. Not that I had either of those, but still, it'd be cool to meet another person with a different taste.

"Nothing bad," she clarified. "I didn't kill anyone or anything like that."

"I wasn't . . . thinking that."

"Okay. Well, anyway, let's not get off track here."

Behind her, Glen stalked the front registers. We were closed and he was taking care of the money.

I put my hand on Kayla's shoulder and guided her into the aisle, out of sight from Glen and his all-seeing eye. I swear that dude was like the Eye of Sauron—he could see everything at all times, even if you were completely hidden down one of the aisles. It made going to the bathroom hard sometimes.

"Glen," I told her, once we were hidden from the front end. She had closed her eyes as if she expected me to move in for a kiss, and more importantly, she didn't back away. I thought all of this was weird, considering we only just met, but then a spike of excitement cut through me. That sensation ended abruptly when I realized even if I wanted to kiss her—and I sort of did—it could never go anywhere. Wouldn't lead to a damn thing. This disappointing realization brought me back down. "The last thing you want Glen to see is you standing around and talking."

"Got it," she said, nodding. "So . . . what is there to do in these parts?"

"Oh, you know. The usual. Bars. Bowling. Movies. There's a laser tag on Route 38. Haven't been in years but—"

"I fucking love laser tag."

I loved that she loved laser tag.

"We should go sometime," I said.

"Tonight?"

I shot her a dubious look, unable to tell if she was kidding or not. "You want to go to laser tag? Tonight?"

She shrugged. "Why not?"

"It's almost ten-thirty. I don't even know if they're open."

"I'll call." She whipped out her phone. Now, if Glen happened to cruise by the aisle and saw Kayla on her phone, doing things that weren't in the Best Tronics employee handbook, like calling other businesses to see if they were open, he'd drag her back to the office and fire her immediately. It was pretty easy to shit-can someone with no tenure around these parts.

I poked my head out of the aisle, locked eyes on Glen. He continued to mess around with the registers, stuffing cash in bags, sending up profit-stuffed envelopes the pneumatic tube system and into the vault.

"Yes, are you still open? You are? Till what time? Midnight? Perfect. Any chance me and my friend can squeeze in a game of laser tag? Yeah? Good, we'll be there in fifteen. Awesome. Thank you so much."

She hung up. I turned to her. She wriggled her eyebrows at me, looking quite proud of herself.

"I guess we're laser tagging?" I asked.

"Oh hell yeah we're laser tagging."

SEVEN

OF course the organizers of laser tag didn't put Kayla and me on the same team. They stuck me on the red team with a bunch of pre-teens who were up way past their bedtime and placed her on the blue team, paired with the demon children's parents. It was 7v7. Before the game started, we huddled in the charging station (each team had a "charging station" on opposite ends of the arena) and listened to the employee, a young girl wearing a referee's uniform, go over the rules–no hitting, no running, no damage to the environment–basically anything other than aiming your gun and shooting your opponents in the designated targets on their electronic vests. When you were low or out of "life", you needed to head back to the charging station to revive yourself. Other than those simple instructions, it was "have fun, kiddos, and for the love of everything that is holy, don't break anything."

The countdown to game time dropped under one minute.

I turned to my teammates. "All right, kids. We really need to win this thing now–"

"Shut up, Frenchie!" one of them yelled.

So perplexed by this nonsensical insult, I couldn't even respond.

Another prepubescent little shit shoved his finger in my face.

"Yeah, shut up, cockmaster!"

"Uh, really?" I asked, glancing at each of them. "That's how you talk to people? Aren't your parents like thirty feet away?"

"Fuck them!" another announced.

"Yeah, they can suck our wangs!"

Animals. I was on a team with a bunch of savage animals who'd clearly been raised by other savage animals. Did I actually talk like that at twelve years old? I decided maybe I had, but I definitely wouldn't verbally assault a complete stranger. These kids had balls.

I decided to keep my mouth shut from here on out, but it was too late—they started shooting me. All of them. At once. They danced around me, leaping about like the flying monkeys in *The Wizard of Oz.* One on them gave me the finger in perpetuity.

I watched my life drain on the indicator on my plastic vest. One of the delightful little turds pointed his gun right at the target in the center of my chest, inches away, and rapidly fired.

Since I never left the station, my backpack started charging again once the life meter hit zero. But still. It was annoying.

In response, I only smiled at him.

"What are you smiling at, pussy-boy?" the kid asked. "I'm gonna make you hurt, fuck-nuts!"

"I'm on your team, you little asshole."

He didn't take too kindly to that. Before I could react, the kid picked his leg up and kicked me directly in the shin. Must have been a goddamn soccer star, the second coming of Pele, because I thought he'd cracked the bone. I dropped to my knees. White spots appeared in front of my vision, which I didn't even know was a real-life thing, just something that had been described in books for dramatic effect, some cute hyperbole. But nope. White spots popped in front of my vision, a heavenly bokeh that swelled and shrunk. Pain shot up my legs, setting fire to my groin area, which I have to admit, concerned me a great deal. Thought maybe the impact ruptured one of my two best friends, a silly notion looking back at it, but at the time, frightened me to no end.

"How'd you like that, titty-fucker?" the kid shouted two inches from my nose. His breath smelled like pizza and orange soda.

I wanted to respond with "not very much, thank you," but I couldn't speak through the shin-splitting pain. I grabbed my gonads out of some sense of comfort.

The countdown dropped to zero and the game had begun. The kids dispersed, running into the arena in search of their parents so they could shoot them, yell obscenities at them, act like the animals they'd been raised to be. On their way to battle, they screamed like a bunch of inmates who had just escaped from an insane asylum.

This was madness. It all felt like dreamlike, strange and beyond the scope of reality.

One of the kids, however, lingered behind and watched me suffer in agony. I used the wall of the charging station to stand up. For a second, I thought the kid stayed back to help me, or at the very least apologize for his friends' behavior—but nope. He pointed at me, laughed, and said, "You suck, bozo!" and then ran off into the game's foggy atmosphere, disappearing amongst the haze.

The pain subsided, vacated my groin area, and the unpleasant feeling lessened with the passage of time. My shin still hurt, but I could walk. Could even run on it if the situation called for it—if a half-dozen villainous little shits aggressively attacked me again.

But I couldn't worry about them. I was here for Kayla. I was here to have fun.

I headed out into the arena. Neon lights bounced off the walls. Loud, crunchy rock music blared through the speakers, something like Nine Inch Nails but on speed. I heard the kids laughing, cursing, most likely destroying the joint, tearing down the walls. Shadows moved in my periphery. I turned and saw one of the parents hiding behind a structural beam designed to fit the theme of the environment, some alien spaceship. They had painted the columns black and carved, into the surface, astrological symbols that glowed a neon green.

I steadied my aim. I didn't think he saw me. He was looking around the corner, keeping an eye out for the kids, the rambunctious terrors that plagued this place. I could tell he saw something in the distance, and he brought the gun up to his eye, aiming.

I had a clear shot at the target on his shoulder. Putting the sights of my weapon to my eye, I locked onto the dude's shoulder.

Then something hit me behind the knee. It took me to the ground. I looked up and saw one of the kids—the one who'd kicked me in the shin—standing over me, the widest smile I'd ever seen on another person's face proudly on display.

"Ha! You fuckin' suck, dickhole!" he shouted down at me, and then bounded off into the shadows of this place.

That was pretty much it for me. I decided all bets were off. I needed to show these monsters they couldn't act like this. Surely their parents never had. Otherwise I wouldn't have been assaulted more in the previous ten minutes than I had in my entire life.

Before I could stand up, another kid streaked past me, slapping me in the face on his way back to the charging station. "Stay down, dick-sneeze!"

Fire burned my eyes.

I felt a hand on my shoulder, and I almost turned around, leading with my fist.

"Whoa!" Kayla said, stepping back. "Dude, are you okay? What the heck happened to you?"

My anger quickly vanished.

"I was . . . nothing, I was . . . I tripped?"

The kids' collective laughter echoed through the place, sounding like a gang of demons hanging out on a street corner in Hell. I heard one of them shout, "Pecker-necker!" and assumed the comment had been directed at me.

Kayla looked at me, clearly knowing I'd avoided the truth.

"Those kids are out-of-control, huh?" she said, her lips spreading into a smile.

"Fucking animals."

"I know, right? One of them elbowed me in the tit. Pretty sure he did it on purpose."

"Which one? I'll kill him." I wasn't joking, but she didn't know that and giggled softly, loud enough that I heard her over the industrial rock.

"Calm down, Rambo. They're just kids."

"Someone should do something about them. Like, their parents, maybe?"

I didn't realize how serious I sounded until she said, "Whoa. They're really getting to you, huh?"

I chewed my tongue, a faint smirk taking control of my lips. "No. No, they're fine. Just a couple of kids being kids. Fun times." I'd spoken through my teeth unintentionally.

"Well, I guess there's only one thing left to do."

"What's that?"

She jammed the gun in my chest and pulled the trigger. My life went down to zero in a matter of three seconds.

"You jerk," I said.

"All is fair in laser tag warfare."

Her brow jumped several times. Then she backtracked, disappearing into the wall of mist behind her, those rolling clouds of faux fog.

Something in my chest moved. My heart. It pumped harder. Faster. I could only smile.

Somewhere nearby, the monsters moved through the shadows.

I decided to recharge.

"Wow," she said, looking at the printout the woman behind the counter gave us. It tallied the scores of each player, down to the finest statistic, like accuracy percentage. "Laser tag is definitely not your game."

"Hard to play when you're getting assaulted by your own teammates every thirty-five seconds."

"Pssh. Yeah. Excuses, excuses." She bumped me with her shoulder. "Admit it. You suck. I'm better than you. And I'm the big winner here tonight."

The stat sheet didn't lie. Kayla was actually the second most valuable player in the whole game. Of course, they ranked me dead last. A pregnant woman in her third trimester outscored me by twenty-five points.

I rolled my eyes. "Okay. I'll let you have this one. Just this once."

"Oh, is that your plan? Let the girl win on the first date? Keep her coming back for more?"

"What? No. Noooooo waaaaaay." Something went off in my head like an M-80. "Wait? Did you say 'date'?"

She shrugged. "Yeah, maybe I did. Does that make it weird now?"

"No. Not at all."

"Do you have a girlfriend or something?"

I couldn't help it. I laughed. "No, no girlfriend."

"Good. Then I have you all to myself."

She walked ahead of me and turned around, started heading toward the parking lot backwards. "I'll even let you buy me ice cream because I'm nice like that."

"Oh, how thoughtful of you."

We got ice cream. And it was the best ice cream had ever tasted.

EIGHT

I rolled up to Percy's curb around five o'clock the next evening. It was cold, but reasonably warm for December near the shore. The temperature had hit the low 50s and was expected to drop fast. I found Percy in his garage along with Hank, a dude who worked the stockroom at Best Tronics. They were watching *The Texas Chainsaw Massacre II* and enjoying some fine local craft brew. They tossed me a sixteen-ounce can as I made my way up the driveway. I'm not the most coordinated dude on the planet, but I made sure I caught that one. The one beer probably cost five bucks.

"Nice catch, Bridges," Hank said, mimicking Glen's voice. I must say, he did an admirable impression of our arch-nemesis.

"Thanks. I guess all those years of being forced to play little league are finally working out for me."

I strolled into the garage and plopped down on one of the lawn chairs, kicked my feet back and cracked open the local brew.

"Where are the 'rents?" I asked. Percy had grown up without a father, like me, but his mother remarried a few years ago. He and his mom moved out of their downtown apartment and into Stephen's home after the ceremony.

"Atlantic City," Percy answered, his eyes remaining glued to the screen. He'd seen the movie a dozen times, but this was how Percy watched movies—he hardly looked away. Anyway, it was almost over. Leatherface did his thing.

"Nice."

Half a beer later, and the closing credits began to roll.

Percy jumped up from his seat. "You," he said, pointing to me like I'd done something terribly wrong. His face betrayed him though, the ghost of a smile touching his lips. "You son of a bitch, you."

I stared at him. Hank grinned foolishly.

Shrugging, I asked, "What in God's name is happening here?"

"Kayla? Dude, what the fuck? Why didn't you tell me?"

I waved him away. "Oh, man. That was nothing. Come on."

"Nothing? Nothing? You took her to play laser tag and get ice cream?"

I froze. "Who the fuck told you that?"

"I worked today, unlike you, and everyone knows already."

I couldn't believe it. Or could I? Rumors always made their way around the store, some quicker than others. But our date had only taken place less than twenty-four hours ago. A new world record for the Best Tronics gossip relay.

"Did Kayla work today?" I asked him.

"I didn't see her."

"Me neither," Hank added. He downed the rest of his beer and cracked open another one.

"Shit. Maybe someone saw us. Or. . ."

"Maybe you have a stalker!" Percy shouted. He proceeded over to the Blu-ray player and ejected the movie. Then he selected two more off the shelf and held them out for us to see. "*The Mutilator* or *The Burning*?"

"*The Burning*, of course," Hank told him. "And what's with you and slashers lately? Seems like that's all you watch."

Percy's face lit up. "I dunno. Maybe it's that whole Hackettstown Hacker situation that's got me in the mood."

Hank and I exchanged glances.

"The Hacketstown who-what?" I asked. Hacketstown was about twenty miles north of us. I'd never heard of such a *situation* happening there until Percy mentioned it. Which made sense; I hardly ever read the local news and barely got on Facebook (my account was set to super private so people couldn't find me—for obvious reasons—and I didn't have much reason to get lost in the rabbit holes of social media).

Percy looked at us like we'd done something unforgivable. "You guys haven't heard of the Hacketstown Hacker?"

We shook our heads.

"Oh, man. It's the craziest thing ever. It's been going on for about month, but we're just starting to get information on it."

"What are you talking about?" I asked, leaning forward.

"Oh, man. Listen to this." He bounced on his toes with pure excitement. "The Hacketstown Hacker, okay, so apparently some guy has been running around the county abducting people and hacking off their limbs. They've actually been keeping it pretty hush-hush, but my cousin works for the Asbury Park Press and he told me all about it. They have this story all ready to go on it, but the police keep trying to shut it down in fear that once the story goes public and everyone knows about it, then the Hacker will stop and they won't be able to catch him. Isn't that fuckin' nuts?"

"Yeah," I said. "That's . . . crazy."

(Okay, I know what you're thinking and no, I am not the Hacketstown Hacker. Not even close. And this isn't one of those stories where at the end it turns out that I AM the Hacketstown Hacker, and you've all been fooled into believing otherwise. Just to be clear: I AM NOT THE HACKETSTOWN HACKER. Okay? Good.)

"I call bullshit," Hank said. "There's no way they can stop the press from going public. What about the safety of the community? We'd all have to know about it if some maniac was on the loose."

"Dude," Percy said, turning to his collection. "*Maniac.* Perfect movie. Which one? Original or remake? Because I love both."

I shook my head. "I don't like how excited you're getting over this Hacker guy. I mean, that's kind of sick, Purse. Hacking people's limbs off? He doesn't kill them, he just . . . takes a limb?"

"Come on. It's interesting. Shit like this never happens on the shore."

"Still calling bullshit on this one," Hank interjected. He cocked his head back and took a big swig of beer.

"It's not bullshit. It's very real. I've done the research. Last night." He put back *The Mutilator* and *The Burning* and grabbed *Maniac,* the 2012 version with Elijah Wood. "There have been several cases of people waking up in strange places with no memory of the last twenty-four hours. And they always wake up missing a limb. Sometimes it's an arm or a leg. Sometimes it's a finger. A toe."

"Someone is actually amputating innocent people?" I asked. It didn't seem possible. And, considering my tour on the amputee meeting circuit, I felt like I would have run into one of these people by now, at a meeting or, at the very least, an online chat. Felt like people *should* be talking about him, this Hacketstown Hacker. I would have caught a whisper somewhere.

I couldn't buy into what Percy was selling, not completely. There had to be something he'd left out or embellished. "How long has this been going on?"

"That's the thing," he said, popping the disc into the player. "They think it's been going on for years. Recently, the Hacker has been doing bigger *jobs,* for the lack of a better term. Ditching fingers and toes in favor of arms and legs. There have been ten victims over the past four years. Two in the last month."

"He's getting careless," I said out loud.

Both of them turned to me like I'd said something totally taboo.

"Sorry. Thinking out loud."

"Anyway," Percy continued, "the police are trying to hold out as long as they can, trying to catch the guy before he goes into hiding. But people are starting to find out about it. Word is getting around. People are talking, like my cousin. I've seen several concerned posts in local Facebook groups. Someone even created a Wordpress page for the Hacker. Complete with newspaper articles about the victims and everything."

I whipped out my phone and ran a quick Google search. Sure enough, Percy wasn't lying. I perused the Wordpress blog about the Hacker, scanning the articles, taking in the information over the course of a minute. I didn't recognize any of the names, not right away. I guess I could have met these people at a meeting. Maybe they were the quiet kind, the folks who weren't ready to talk about their incidents, who weren't ready to *share.* No one ever forced anyone to share—that was forbidden—but eventually everyone came around. But what if they didn't? Or . . . what if they lied? I also supposed they could have used fake names, something I considered when I first started sneaking into meetings. The main reason I refused to use a fake name was I'd already felt shitty about lying. Using an alias would have made me feel even more like a scumbag. Not the smartest decision I'd ever made. I mean, I'd taken my efforts that far, why not go all out, right? But I couldn't. I couldn't step that far outside myself, if that makes any sense. It does to me.

I ran my finger down the list of victims. The most recent: a woman by the name of Wendy Adams.

I pulled up Facebook and searched the name.

"Holy shit," I said out loud. My stomach tumbled. The center of my chest fluttered.

Both of them glanced over at me, deeply concerned with the look they saw on my face.

"Dude, what the hell?" Percy held his arms out, awaiting an explanation. "Are you okay?"

Wendy Adams, the woman I'd slept with last week, stared up at me from my phone. She was smiling. Her eyes held not a speck of sadness, unlike when I met her. She looked happy in this photograph, which had obviously been taken pre-incident.

The incident.

Wendy had told me—told the group—that she'd been sideswiped by a drunk driver. That had been a lie. In actuality, she had been the latest victim of the Hacketstown Hacker.

"Hello?" Hank said, snapping his fingers right in front of my face.

Alert, I looked up from my phone. "What? What happened?"

"You zoned out on us, dude," Percy said. He'd pressed play on the remote; the movie was already a few minutes in. On screen, Elijah Wood admired himself in front of a mirror.

"Sorry. I . . . I can't believe this is a real thing."

Percy found his smile. "Kind of cool, right? I mean, it's sick, and I totally feel bad for these women."

Women. I didn't realize that all the victims had been women until Percy said so.

". . .but," he said, "I dunno. Is it wrong to think this is kinda neat?"

"Yes," I told him. "Yes, it is wrong. These women's lives are being ruined. They'll never be the same again. Do you know how much therapy it will take for them to get over something like this? Countless hours. And you know what? They'll never *get over it.* Not completely. They're damaged. Permanently." I didn't realize how angry I had sounded until I asked, "And you want to celebrate that?"

Hank dropped his gaze, fixating on the garage floor.

Percy took a gulp of air, clearly embarrassed. "I'm sorry, Ray. I didn't know you felt so strongly about . . . about this. I totally get it, though. I don't think it's a great thing, it's just . . . I don't know. Unusual. And you know how I find shit like this interesting."

I didn't mean to explode like that. I let my anger simmer for a moment. Percy didn't actually believe this stuff was cool. The inner workings of a psychopath's mind fascinated him on some morbid level. Nothing more. Not like he admired the killer or aspired to be him.

Not a killer, though, is he? No, technically he wasn't. According to the articles I had skimmed, not one of his victims had ever died. He'd cut off limbs and that was all. Stitched them up and dumped them off somewhere, in a public place so they'd be found. Found and taken somewhere where they could receive the proper medical attention. So they could live.

"It's fine. I'm sorry. I didn't mean to make it a big deal. It's just . . ." I sipped my beer. "I don't think it's something we should celebrate."

"Okay. I get that." He hit the power button on the television, killing the showing of *Maniac.*

We drank the rest of the craft beer and spoke very little. When I left, the mood more or less stayed the same, not that awkward but still a little bit, and I told them both I'd see them tomorrow at work.

NINE

I kept trying to *not* think about the Hacketstown Hacker, the fact Wendy had been the latest victim and lied about it, that someone out there was knocking off the limbs of innocent people, creating the very scenarios that got me off. It was sick and I felt disgusted about the whole thing. I'd never once been embarrassed about my kink (if that's what you want to call it), at least not to myself, but inside, now, I felt ashamed. Like my methods were wrong, that somehow I was an accomplice to this mess, and I needed to change, correct myself. Like I needed to start training my mind to find people with a full set of limbs attractive. To find able-bodied people sexy, something that seemed impossible.

Maybe *I* was the permanently damaged one. Maybe I'm a monster, after all.

I walked into work and it felt like the place had a black cloud hanging over it. I knew it was just me and not the place, but still, everything felt skewed. Slanted. About ready to slide off the edge of the world and into a murky abyss.

Percy greeted me before anyone else. "Dude, I'm sorry about yesterday. I didn't mean to come off as a dick."

"It's fine," I said, patting him on the back. "Sorry I got so sensitive about it."

"No, you were right to. I shouldn't have glorified what some nutjob is doing out there." He shook his entire body as if a chill had crawled up his spine. "Sometimes this horror stuff gets the best of me."

"Don't worry about it." I scanned the front end. Two cashiers were chatting with each other, laughing. No signs of customers or management. "Is Kayla here?"

"Haven't seen her. Check the daily lineup, though. I thought I saw her name on there."

"Will do."

I walked over to the greeter's podium where they kept the daily lineup. Sharlene leaned there in her usual pose, waiting for customers to enter and exit. She smiled at me as I approached, then went back to chewing her mouthful of gum. I peeked at the lineup, saw Kayla was due in a little bit later.

"Checking on your girlfriend?" Sharlene asked.

"Girlfriend? What? No."

"Not what I heard, lover-boy."

"Are you goddamn kidding me?"

Blowing a bubble, she shook her head. "Nope. Heard you two went out for ice cream the other night. So, when's the wedding? Better get an invite."

I rolled my eyes. "It's not like that."

"Oh no?"

"No."

"Are you sure?"

"Positive."

"You don't think she's cute?"

"I didn't say that."

"What are you saying?"

"That we're just friends. Nothing more."

"Not what she thinks."

"How do you know what she thinks?"

She shrugged nonchalantly. "I dunno. Maybe we talk."

"What's that mean, 'maybe we talk'?"

"It means, maybe she tells me stuff, doofus."

"Doofus? Doofus? How old are we, Sharlene?"

"I'm nineteen and shut up."

"Okay, so what did she tell you?"

A knowing smile broke out across Sharlene's face, and I knew she was either putting me on or she had actually spoken with Kayla. My desperation skewered me.

"She said she likes you, man."

"Did she really say that, Sharlene?"

"Calling me a liar, James VanderGeek?"

"James Vander– Look, did she say it or not?"

She wrinkled her nose and shrugged. "Ask her yourself."

"Oh goddammit, Sharlene."

She held up the small watch that usually stayed with the greeter's podium. "Better punch the clock, Brad Shit. Glen is on a roll this morning. He's in Super Dick Mode, so watch out. Guy needs to get laid or something. Wound up like a yo-yo."

I opened my mouth to say something witty, but then thought better of it. "Thanks for your advice, Sharlene," came out instead.

"No problem, Bro Namath."

I strolled over to the break room, counting down the minutes until I saw Kayla again.

Kayla crossed the entrance's threshold in five minutes before her shift. I waited by the front door, pretending to talk to a customer on the phone about their current cell phone plan. She waved at me as she walked by, lifting her dark sunglasses from her face. I waved back and wondered how goofy I looked doing so. I couldn't remember the last time I waved at someone.

"Yes, well," I said, talking into the phone (pretending to), "if you change your mind, please be sure to give us a call. K, bye."

I shoved the phone back in my hip holster and caught up to Kayla, who headed toward the back.

"Hey," I said.

"Oh, hey," she replied, flashing that smile. "What's up?"

"Nothing. How are you?"

"Great."

"That's . . . great."

God, I'm terrible at talking to people. You never truly know how awkward you are until you try to hold a conversation about nothing.

"So. . ."

"So. . ."

"The other night," I started to say, making sure we were out of range from the other employees. Specifically Glen. I didn't know if he'd like the fact I'd hung out with the new girl, especially the one he assigned me to train. I assumed there was nothing wrong with the nature of our relationship, no corporate rule stating otherwise. But still, he judged people past what the company's guidelines suggested. Glen had his own set of rules. His own way of doing things.

"Our date?"

The way she spoke made it sound so official.

"Is that what it was?" I asked, my throat narrowing to the diameter of a drinking straw.

"Wasn't it?" Her coy smile shredded my nerves. My organs had turned to jelly.

"I . . . I didn't know."

"Well, now you do."

She acted like it wasn't a big deal. Like us having a date was a casual thing, something ordinary.

Then I thought, *Well, maybe it isn't a big deal.* Maybe I was making a big deal of it. Maybe that's just what normal twenty-somethings and thirty-somethings do. Maybe that was what people with*out* strange sexual desires do.

I never felt more like a freak. Thirty-two years old and I acted like an eighth-grader who'd taken the hottest girl from class to the movies.

"Yeah, of course," I said, trying to match her confidence level and completely failing. I even hit my forehead with the heel of my palm. "A date. I knew that."

"Really? Because you just said you didn't."

"I did?" I didn't even know what I was saying anymore. This was nuts. My neck felt like a fire.

She stopped, spun around. Faced me. She peered into my eyes, the playful smile now gone. "You're not going to get weird on me, are you?"

"Me? Weird? Uh, no."

"Because the truth is, Raymond, I like you."

She fucking called me Raymond. I didn't even mind it. I hated my full name, *hated it,* but coming off her lips it sounded like the best name in the world.

"But don't get weird on me. Please don't do that. You won't, will you?"

I shook my head. "Nope. Won't do that."

"Good." She smiled again. "I gotta punch in. Talk later?"

"Of course."

She headed toward the time clock, and I stood there, still, watching, realizing how fucked this situation was and how badly it would all end.

TEN

SEX complicates things. Right? Relationships would be perfect without it. But they also wouldn't. Because people need sex. Right? Chemically, it balances them out, releases endorphins or something. And when you do it with someone you love, it's a million times better because now you're emotionally invested in that person and you get to share something beautiful with them. Sex without love is just sex, nothing more than a couple of naked, writhing bodies trying to hump toward the finish line, trying to achieve that state of maximum pleasure—those ten precious seconds where nothing in the world matters except that overwhelming rush of euphoria. Sex without love is just sex and that's fine, because after all, I've engaged in my fair share of meaningless fucking.

But I can't say I ever loved someone.

After our first date, I didn't love Kayla. Least I don't think I did. But there was something there. Something tugged at me, something crawled inside my bones and made me feel funny things. Something in my heart made it beat just a little harder. Faster. Slightly out of tune with the rest of my body. Butterflies in the stomach when I was around her and all that.

I tried to limit my feelings, reel them in, because I saw where this train was headed before it pulled into the station. I couldn't have sex with Kayla because physically, I wasn't attracted to her. She wasn't my type. My *type* was amputees, and Kayla's body carried all her bones. It wasn't the end of the world. I've met women I've connected with on a personal level whose limbs were all attached. It was no big deal. I just distanced myself. Stayed away from them. Talked to them less. Eventually those small feelings faded and they moved onto someone else, someone who paid them more attention, someone who could give them the things I could not.

But something told me I couldn't do that with Kayla. There was something about her, something special, and—as corny as this sounds—I didn't think I could quit on her. I didn't think I could abandon my feelings as I had in the past.

So then I thought this: maybe, just maybe, I could make an exception. That whatever psychological defect my brain had, whatever *thing* prevented me from being sexually attracted to able-bodied women, maybe I could put that on hold just this once. Because of my feelings. Because of how I felt about her. Because of our rare connection.

But also, maybe that wouldn't happen. Maybe I would fail her. Maybe I shouldn't even try.

A whirlwind of possibilities and conflicting thoughts fought for head space.

She had told me not to get weird on her, but the more I thought about our situation, the stranger my ideas became. For a second, I thought about telling her about my preferences. That maybe, if she loved me enough, she'd take a finger off. Maybe a toe. Not as sexy, but it could work. If she truly loved me, maybe she'd shed an arm. Or a leg.

The thoughts, tantalizing as they were, also disgusted me. Which, I don't know, was maybe a sign. A sign I could make this work, I could engage in a meaningful relationship with an able-bodied woman.

This was progress.

But who was I kidding? It was gonna be a complete disaster.

We went out a few times after our little talk. To the movies. A diner. There was an indoor mini-golf place in the next town over. We went there before a nice meal at Jack's Seafood, the best and fanciest place in the area, at least within my budget. This dating game was hell on my wallet. I had already burned through my weekly spending money and began dipping into my rent money. I knew it wouldn't be too much of a problem. Worst-case scenario, I'd pull from the "college" account, the small stash my mother set aside in case I ever decided to return to school someday. She'd only contributed a couple grand to it, and throughout the years, I had never touched a dollar.

After dinner, we walked along the boardwalk, under the winter moon. It was cold, *freezing* in fact, and no one else in town was crazy enough to stroll the boards on thirty-degree nights. We held hands. We talked. We laughed.

We kissed.

The first kiss happened like this: she turned to me on a dime, threw her face in my face, and pressed her lips against mine. We engaged in a powerful kiss, the kind where your lips feel like they're trapped beneath the tire of a parked car, an enormous swell of pressure. I kissed back just as passionately. Sandwiched our faces together as if we were one face. Soon after our tongues got involved. There wasn't a lot of tongue, but just enough, just a taste. We both had seafood breath and I could taste the shrimp and scallops on her just as she tasted my mussels and clams. After thirty seconds of what the old folks might call "necking" we mutually parted. Pulled back. Stared at each other's eyes.

"Damn," she said. "You can kiss."

"As can you."

Neither of us wanted that moment to end, and we dove back in for our second kiss. It was shorter, didn't have as much weight behind the force, more like a gentle meeting of soft flesh, but the touch channeled the same spark. I wrapped my arms around her and pulled her close. She threw her arms around my neck. Our knees aligned in a row, our legs became a wall. We rubbed them together for warmth and comfort.

None of this turned me on. But I did feel something in my chest; something moved and spread and crawled through me, a type of energy that almost felt like a good drug, polluting my senses—not sure if that was "love" but it felt close enough.

Holy shit, I thought, *I'm falling for her. This is what falling feels like.* And then I knew why they called it "falling in love." The sensation of leaping off a skyscraper and plummeting toward the concrete walk circumnavigated my entire body.

We smooched a little while longer, then the cold became too much.

She grabbed my hands, squeezed. "Take me home."

"Already?" I looked at my cell. "It's only a quarter after nine."

"Not mine," she told me, arching her eyebrows. "Yours."

The clothes came off pretty quickly, the scene set like the movies—the couple comes busting through the door, kissing each other, aggressively caressing each other, peeling the layers off one by one in a fury. Cut to various undergarments sailing through the air. Jump cut to the living room's unoccupied corner, only to see it filled with needless articles. It was a lot like that. Okay, maybe it was *exactly* like that. Anyway, in under a minute we made our way to the bedroom, were on the bed, naked, continuing to smash our lips together.

"Do you have a condom?" she asked and continued gently nibbling on my ear.

I reached over into the nightstand and grabbed one. My erection was only halfway there, so I had some work to do. I laid the semen catcher on the pillow next to her. Then I went down on her. She grabbed a handful of my hair and moaned. As I did my thing, I noticed I wasn't getting any harder. If anything, I was shrinking. The snake was retreating back into its cave.

This can't be happening, I thought.

But what did I expect? I had to know this was how it would end. Earlier I told you I'd tried to have sex with able-bodied women before—not once had it ever worked out. Did I really think Kayla would be any different?

The answer is *yes.* Yes, I absolutely did.

I thought the spark between us would ignite and spread fire, but that wasn't the case. The spark had caught fire but my stupid body had been there with an extinguisher. And in case you didn't get that analogy, the fire was my dick.

"What's the matter?" she asked, now working my lower half with her mouth.

"I don't know."

She tried again but I stayed as soft as a new sock.

"Ray . . ."

"I don't know . . ."

After a few minutes of nothing working, she drew back, immediately hopping off the bed.

"I'm sorry," was the only thing I could say.

"It's fine." She was clearly pissed, and had every right to be.

She stormed over to the corner of the room, picked up her clothes, and started putting them back on.

"I . . . I don't know what happened." I felt like I needed to lie. To cover it up. Throw a Band-Aid over the situation. I didn't even think this could be the beginning of the end for me, because of this everyone would find out about my bizarre sexual condition. I kept these issues far from my mind; I'd have plenty of time to panic about that later. Right now, I wanted to make her feel better. Make it so she didn't feel like she failed. Shame and embarrassment were scribbled all over her face. She hid it well, her expression featureless and lax. But the uncomfortableness post-failure was palpable, strong, living inside us both.

"It's fine," she said, and I almost believed her.

"It's never happened to me before."

"Okay." She hiked her jeans up over her hips. "It's probably just me. I don't . . . *do it* for you, I guess."

"No, it's not that."

She had been preparing to throw her shirt on when she stopped, looked at me. It was the first time we'd made eye contact since the failure to launch. "No? Then what was it?"

I wanted to tell her everything. I wanted to come clean. I wanted the truth out there, I wanted the whole situation to roll off my tongue. It had felt good confessing to Wendy in the supermarket, and I knew it would feel a hundred times better confiding in Kayla–you know, because of how I felt about her. But in the end, I just couldn't do it. And I knew why. It was the fear, fear she wouldn't understand, fear she would label me a "freak", fear she would never speak to me again and tell everyone what a terrible monster I was.

(I am not a monster.)

"I don't know. Just . . . a thing."

"A thing?" She threw her shirt on. Once dressed, she grabbed her purse off my dresser. "A thing?"

"It won't happen again." Another lie. Rolled off quite naturally. Too naturally. But she had none of it.

"You're right about that."

She speed-walked toward the front door, not waiting for me to catch up and show her out. Slamming the door shut, she left without saying goodbye. Without a goodnight kiss.

But she did leave *with* something. My heart.

My *fucking* heart.

ELEVEN

I dreaded going into work the next day. I had sick time, sure, but what would that help except delay the inevitable. I'd have to face her eventually. Unless she quit Best Tronics, which, judging by the embarrassment etched in her face as she stormed out of my apartment, was quite possible. Maybe she was more embarrassed about people finding out than I was.

I strolled in fifteen minutes early—a rarity—and headed straight for the greeter's station.

"Lineup," I said.

"Well," Debra the greeter said, scrunching her face at me, "someone's in a crabby mood this morning."

That was true. Super crabby. And I also didn't care. I grabbed the lineup from her and scanned the sheet. According to the lineup, Kayla already punched in. She should have been in appliances by now, training.

I thanked Debra and hurried over to the appliance department.

Didn't take long to spot Kayla—she was standing next to Ken, the department manager, with a smile on her face as he ran through the features of some GE model. A great big smile ate up most of his face too, and the two seemed to be having a grand old time.

Great.

A flash of jealousy temporarily consumed me.

"Hey, Ken," I said, approaching, waving at them. "Hey, Kayla. Can I borrow you for a moment?"

"Borrow me?" she asked, still smiling, though the strength of that smile had taken a hit once she saw me.

"Yeah, just need to talk for a second."

Ken shot me an odd look like I had broken up a dinner date and not some meaningless work conversation. "We're kind of in the middle of something, Ray."

"Yeah, I know. It'll only take a minute."

Ken rolled his eyes, but then gave me permission with a dismissive wave.

Kayla followed me down the aisle, around the corner. I turned to her, my eyes pleading for forgiveness.

"I'm so sorry about last night," was the first thing I said. My hands were folded in prayer. Didn't know if that would help or hurt, but seemed apropos for the situation at hand. "It was a fucked-up thing that happened."

Her eyes bulged. "Yeah, you think?"

"How can I make it up to you?"

She glanced around, making sure no one was watching our semi-secret rendezvous. "I don't know if you can." Her voice was above a whisper, but not by much. "Do you know how embarrassed I am? Do you have any idea?"

I searched for the right thing to say, but I knew anything other than the truth was the *wrong* thing to say.

But still. I couldn't do it. I couldn't admit what actually happened.

"None of what happened was your fault," I told her.

"Am I not attractive? Are you gay?"

"Yes, you're attractive. No, I'm not gay."

"Do you jerk off too much?"

I almost laughed.

"Happened to this guy I was seeing. He jerked off like twenty times a day. When it came to me, there was just nothing left. I think he was addicted to porn and—"

"I don't jerk off too much."

She glared at me. "Then. What. Is it?"

"I don't know. Nerves?"

"Nerves?"

"Yeah, look. I really like you. And I just wanted things to be perfect and I wanted you to like me and I wanted it to be special. I guess I was overthinking it. Kinda psyched myself out."

"Psyched yourself out?"

"Yeah." It was the best excuse I could come up with under pressure. "Psyched myself out." At least it sounded convincing. Or maybe what I told her was total horseshit and transparent and I had just become an expert at lying, which was why it sounded so good and . . . and *true*.

"So what're you saying?"

My eyes shifted. "That . . . I . . . want to try again?"

She only stared. I waited for her to hit me. Kick me in the scrotum. Any reaction was preferable over her glare, though. Her eyes carved trenches into me.

"Try again?" she asked. I opened my mouth to explain, but she beat me to it. "Ray, I don't think I could go through that again. I mean, what if *it* happens a second time. It'll ruin me forever."

"Trust me. One more date. No pressure. We don't have to try again, but let's hang out and see how the night goes. Okay? Dinner and a movie at my place?"

She arched her back and nodded at Ken, who had checked his watch every thirty seconds or so. "One minute, Ken," she told him, then leaned into me. Her lips hovered a few inches from me, so close I could feel her breath tickle my ear canal. "One more date. No pressure. Tomorrow night. Your place."

She kissed my cheek, then disappeared down the aisle. I heard her apologizing to Ken, saying how important our conversation was and it wouldn't happen again; he now had her undivided attention. She continued to smile that smile, that cute pose everyone adored. And fuck, how could you not?

I turned and headed toward the back, conjuring up ways to make sure what happened last night would never, *ever* happen again.

Viagra.

I stared at Percy, wanting to say something, but found I had nothing on the subject. Except, "Viagra?"

"Yeah, man. The little blue pill. It'll clear up your . . . *situation.*"

We were wiping down the appliances. It was almost closing time and the store was completely dead, so we told Ken we'd help him out with closing duties. It gave me time to explain my situation to Percy, the only person in this store—heck, the whole world—I felt comfortable discussing "sex stuff" with. No, I didn't tell him about the acrotomophilia or anything like that in the slightest, but I did tell him about Kayla and last night and how I couldn't . . . uh, *perform.* I gave him the same story I'd handed Kayla earlier—chalked it up to nerves and all that.

"You'll get a boner no matter what with that stuff," he explained. "There's no shame in having a little ED. Happens to everyone once in a while. I mean, not me. But you know. I've read on the Internet—"

"Well, isn't that shit astronomically expensive?"

He shrugged. "I don't know. Never bought the shit."

"Don't I need a prescription?"

A coy smile conquered his face. "Or know someone who has a stash."

"You know someone?" I asked incredulously.

"Hell yeah. My stepdad has a bottle of the stuff in the top drawer of his dresser. I *borrowed* twenty bucks from him once, a few years back . . . okay, more like a few months back and technically he didn't know about it, so I guess I stole it. But I saw the stuff when I was going through his shit."

"Interesting."

"Yeah, so, I guess he won't notice if a pill or two is missing. I mean, he never said anything about the twenty bucks."

"Okay." I shrugged. Honestly, I didn't hate the idea. If nothing else, maybe this would buy me a little time until I figured things out. Until I figured out how to cure myself.

Cure yourself? I thought. *How can you cure yourself when you're not sick?*

"Let's do it," I told him.

"Perfect. Swing by tomorrow before work. I'll have it for you."

Percy delivered on his promise. Right before my date with Kayla, I popped a pill.

An hour later, halfway through *Stand By Me,* I pitched a tent so large it fucking hurt.

I was ready to go.

And go I went.

TWELVE

"THAT was incredible," she said, plopping her head down on the pillow beside me. "It was . . . it was . . . it was just great."

"I'm glad you thought so." My heart hammered at a thousand beats per minute. I didn't think it should be beating that quickly, but I guess I had the little blue pill to thank for that. "I enjoyed it too, in case you were wondering."

"I wasn't," she said, giggling. She rolled over and kissed my cheek, then spooned me.

We fell asleep after that. Didn't wake up until the next morning.

We were both off, and over breakfast at IHOP, we decided to take a trip to the mall in Monmouth County, peruse the shops. Maybe take in a movie. There wasn't much else to do on a Thursday in December—a dreary, December day nonetheless, complete with gray skies and threats of snowfall.

The whole morning I felt awful about the previous night. I mean, don't get me wrong, the sex was wonderful, even if I wasn't completely into it or attracted to her. I had gone through the motions, so to speak. But it was more of the connection, that internal flare captivated me, made me enjoy it. My orgasm was routine, but that was because I couldn't stop looking at her arms and legs, trying to imagine them gone. It was distracting. But I managed. And she enjoyed herself, and in the end, that was all that mattered. That was why I went along with Percy's suggestion in the first place.

But I had to come clean.

I couldn't hide it from her. If we were going to date, invest in a meaningful relationship, it shouldn't start with lies. I couldn't tell her about the acrotomophilia, but I could at least tell her I took Viagra in order to seal the deal.

"I have to admit something to you," I said, just as the waiter brought us stacks and stacks of pancakes.

She froze like I was about to tell her I had Hep-C or something. "Do I want to know?"

"I feel like I should tell you. Be honest with you."

"What is it?" Her tone was sharp. She braced herself for bad news. I tried to make it sound worse than it was, build it up that way. Then maybe she wouldn't be mad.

"Before you came over last night, I popped a Viagra."

She glared at me. "A Viagra?"

"Yeah, you know, so it wouldn't happen again."

"But why would it happen again?"

"I'm not saying it would have, but I wanted to be sure. There was a lot of pressure, and I didn't want to drop the ball. I didn't want to . . . you know, lose you."

A faint smile played on her lips. "That's kind of sweet."

"You're not mad?"

She shrugged. "I wish you would have told me, sure. Also, wish you didn't need it to have sex with me, but . . . I guess I understand. Sex can be so psychological sometimes, you know?"

Oh, I knew. I didn't tell her how much I knew.

"But I'm not furious." She leaned in. "You're not going to use it every time, though, are you?"

"No, definitely not. I'm hoping the nerves are behind me."

"Good." She took my hands. "I'm happy you told me. You're very honest. A lot of guys wouldn't admit that to someone they just started dating."

"Oh, we're dating now, are we?"

Her forehead creased. "Are you kidding me?"

I laughed. We kissed over the pancakes.

Things were great.

But the fact still remained . . . I wasn't physically attracted to her. I couldn't take the blue pills forever. And I couldn't make love to her without them.

I would have to fix that. *Fix* me.

But I couldn't, because I wasn't broken.

And if I couldn't fix me, then I'd have to fix *her*.

As we ate, an old man in the booth next to us flipped through his newspaper. The headline on the front page read, "MISSING WOMAN FOUND ALIVE: THE HACKETSTOWN HACKER STRIKES AGAIN."

And that was when the idea came to me.

Maybe I could fix Kayla after all.

THIRTEEN

I am not a monster.

I kept telling myself that, but the more I thought about *fixing* Kayla, the less inclined I was to believe this personal anthem. My thoughts were crazy, buzzing between my ears like bees in a hive come springtime. I kept thinking about the Hacketstown Hacker and what he'd done to that local girl. I wondered if I had the stones to do something like that to Kayla—and, every time one of these sick thoughts popped into my head, I puked. I tried to push them out. Send them away. Think of something else on the fly, but each time the disgusting images flashed before me, a frenzy of scenes including me and Kayla—me with a hatchet in hand, going to work on one of her arms.

I just got finished puking into a garbage can behind Best Tronics when Percy rounded the corner.

"Dude, what the hell?" He backed away from me. "You got the flu?"

I wiped my mouth on a paper towel and threw it in with the puke. "No. Bad sushi."

"Told you to stop eating that shit."

"Can't help it. It's so delicious."

"You're gonna die of salmonella one of these days."

"Yeah . . ."

(Kayla. Naked. On the bed. Me. Chainsaw in my hands. Motor cranking. Chain zipping. The hungry teeth moving closer to her exposed flesh. Panic in her eyes. Sheer terror. Freckles of blood dotting her face as the saw shreds through skin, muscle, and bone.)

I tossed the rest of my stomach into the garbage can. I didn't think there had been anything left, but my body proved me wrong.

"What the fuck, man!" Percy jumped back a few feet, making sure the vomit didn't splash his shoes.

"Sorry." One more violent, chunky stream exploded forth. Some of it speckled the side of the building, but I hardly cared. As long as Glen wasn't skulking about. Seeing him was the last thing I needed. He'd probably bring me to the office to administer a drug and alcohol test. "Last one, I promise."

It *had* to be the last of it. My body left nothing inside my stomach. Everything had been purged. I never felt so depleted in all my life.

"Nasty," said Percy as he pinched shut his nose. "Smells like old, moldy cheese and dead ferrets."

"That's fucking gross."

"You're fucking gross."

I didn't have anything left to wipe my mouth with, so I used my sleeve.

"I'm gonna tell Glen I got sick and head home."

He smirked as if he knew I had alternative plans. "You're going to hang out with Kayla, aren't you?"

"No, definitely not."

"Why?" His expression suddenly changed, as if I'd crushed his spirit somehow. "Is everything okay between you two?"

"Yeah, great." By *great* I meant things were going okay. On the surface, everything was fantastic. We were still seeing each other every other night. Still banging. When things did end up getting intimate, I made sure to break off a piece of the blue pill just to ensure I wouldn't have issues. I didn't tell her I was still using the boner juice and she didn't ask. If she had . . . I dunno, maybe I would have lied. I was seriously considering chopping off one of her limbs in the name of love—hiding the boner pills from her was the least of my worries now.

It'd been a week and a half and things were going smoothly. Only on the surface, though. Underneath, I was a wreck.

"Great is good," he said, peeking around, in search of other degenerate employees.

"Yeah, so, if you could cover for me this afternoon, that'd be great."

"Sure, man. Whatever you need."

I walked away in search of Glen, or whatever manager I was able to report to.

"Oh, hey," Percy called, "having another horror movie night on Saturday. You and Kayla should stop on by."

I told him I'd think about it.

I lay in bed, thoughts swimming. The sick images did not pass, didn't even slow down. The Hacketstown Hacker was in my head now. He showed me all the things we could do to Kayla, to make her *right.* To make her fuckable without the blue pills.

I dry heaved the rest of the afternoon. When she called, I picked up and told her my fever had spiked, causing headaches and nausea, and I had to bail on tonight's plans—pizza and movies at my place. She understood, offered to bring me something. Medicine. A bottle of cola. Chicken noodle soup. Anything at all. I declined. I was in love with the girl, but I didn't want to see her face right now. It felt wrong to.

I needed to fix this. *Fix me.* Not *fix her.* There was nothing wrong with her. She was perfect. I was the demented one. The one who had these terrible thoughts, who conjured scenarios where I shaved a limb off her in order to please my penis. I was sick. *I* needed help.

I am not a monster.

Yes you are.

Like a colony of ants, these thoughts infested me. I couldn't tune them out. I tried to think about other things. I thought of Kayla in the laser tag arena *(limping around the dark on one leg)* and I thought of Kayla ringing up a customer *(her mechanical hand keying in the numbers)* and I thought of Kayla underneath me during sex *(wrapping one arm around my neck because the other was gone, missing, never coming back)* and I thought of Kayla smiling,

smiling because she was happy.

I looked down and realized I was hard.

I rolled my eyes.

I needed to make a choice. A difficult choice. Either break it off or break off a piece of her. Those were my options. I had to be real with myself—nothing about my condition (my preference) would ever change. It'd been so deeply rooted in my brain, hard-wired in. No shrink could ever undo what had been done. It was just the way it was. The way *I* was.

So I had to break it off with her.

Leave her.

Tell her it wasn't working out.

But I couldn't. Because I was in love. I had searched for this feeling since going to support group meetings and combing DisabledMeets.com. I had always hoped to find *the one*, corny as that sounds, but it was true. All I ever wanted was to truly love somebody, connect with them in a way I never had with any other human being.

And that person was Kayla.

She was perfect. On the inside. On the outside, one minor amendment and she'd be everything I've ever dreamed of and more. I could picture her walking down the aisle in a white dress, the plastic hand at the end of a prosthetic arm holding a bouquet of beautiful flowers. And she'd be smiling, with no trace of underlying sadness.

That was the dream.

But right now, it had developed into a nightmare.

I had to make a choice.

And so I did.

There was no way I could leave a love like ours behind. No matter what, I had to see this through to the end.

I needed to destroy her.

FOURTEEN

PERCY gaped at me, horrified and intrigued all at once. "You want to do what now?"

I sighed, then took another sip of beer. "I know it sounds absolutely nuts, but now that you understand my situation, you know where I'm coming from, right?"

A few minutes prior, I told Percy everything. My strange taste for amputated women. Me and Kayla's blossoming romance. The true reason behind my erectile dysfunction. And how I planned to correct that.

It was a gamble. Figured it would go over one of two ways. One, he'd be on board, maybe offer some suggestions. He was into horror movies, not that that made him as twisted as my thoughts, but I figured he could tap into his creativity and offer up a bit of advice. On the other hand, he could call the cops on me.

For a second, I leaned hard on the latter.

"I mean, it's sick as fuck, but yeah, I guess I do." His eyes expanded. "Holy shit, that's why you never talked about girls." He chuckled, shook his head as if this were something he should have seen coming.

"Bravo, you cracked the case."

"It all makes so much sense now." He spent a few seconds trying to wrap his brain around it, piecing together the puzzle I'd scattered before for him over the last eight years or so. "Shit, man. How come you didn't tell me about this earlier?"

"Embarrassed, I guess."

"What's there to be embarrassed about? If anyone could understand this, it's me."

"How's that?"

"Because I like weird shit."

"That's true."

"Now I know why you freaked out a couple weeks back. When we were watching *Maniac*."

"I may have overreacted a bit."

He flicked his hand at me. "No, you were right. But I have to say, why the sudden change of heart?"

Tilting my head sideways, I said, "I don't follow."

"Well, a couple weeks ago you were all like 'we shouldn't celebrate people destroying other people', and now you're literally about to hack a limb off some chick you dig."

He had a solid point. "It's different now."

"How so?"

"Because."

"Because how?"

"It just is, Purse."

"That's a shitty answer."

"You know why."

"I want to hear you say it."

I hung my head, still unsure if I wanted to travel down this road. There was still plenty of time to turn around. Plenty of time to keep these thoughts, these disturbing notions, as they were—just thoughts and nothing more. "Love," I said, looking him straight in the eyes. "I love her, man. So very much."

"*Love*." He shrugged. "So love changes everything, huh?"

I nodded. "Absolutely. Love changes everything."

"You're really into this girl."

I rolled my eyes in a *haven't-you-been-paying-attention* manner. "She's the one, man."

"Oh, she's the *one*." His eyebrows twitched in succession, mocking me. "Fancy."

"Stop it. You going to help me or not?"

He grimaced. "I don't know, man. I love horror and I love watching people get mutilated on the screen. I'm just not into real-life violence. And I can assure you I'm not into murdering people."

"We're not murdering anyone."

"Yeah, but you know . . . close enough."

"Two weeks ago, you were admiring the Hacketstown Hacker's handiwork." I finished my beer, crushed the can, tossed it into the garbage, then folded my arms across my chest. "Now you're all like 'oh, I don't like violence. Violence is bad.'"

"First of all, I don't sound like that." He cracked open another beer and sipped the foamy rush that bubbled at the mouth of the can. "Secondly, I like living in an imaginary setting."

"The Hacketstown Hacker is real."

"Yeah, but that shit won't happen to me. I can enjoy it from the distance. As an observer. Getting too close to something like that . . . I don't know, man. Kinda freaks me out. I like it as a fantasy."

"Yeah, but it *is* real. He's out there. Hacking. The latest victim was taken right here. In our town."

"Then I don't know what you want me to tell you. Go ask him to take part in your little love mission. Maybe he'll lend you a hand."

We both paused. I curled my lip at him.

"Okay," he said, pointing at me, "that pun was totally intentional and I won't apologize for it."

"You know what?" My lips now formed a smile. A knowing smile. A terrible one.

"Oh God, what?"

"That's a genius idea."

"What's a genius idea?"

"The Hacketstown Hacker."

"Oh shit, Ray, I was joking. I was making a joke. I wasn't fucking serious. Wait, you can't be fucking serious. Can you? Are you serious right now? I hate your face, Ray. Don't look at me with that face."

"We can find him."

"No, no we can't. The police can't find him, how the hell are we going to?"

He had a point. "I don't know. We have leads."

"Leads?"

"Wendy, this woman I met from one of the meetings. She was one of the victims."

Percy covered his mouth. "Did you . . . you know . . . bang her?"

"We had sex, yes."

"Ew, man. This is starting to get too weird, even for me."

"You know, you're really surprising me." I pointed to his black t-shirt. "For someone who's wearing a *Mutilator* shirt, I thought you'd be into this."

"Totally different. Told you. It's, like, totally real now. And freaking me out. Look at this." He showed me his arm; gooseflesh covered every visible inch.

"Anyway, we can at least try. Maybe figure out his patterns. Track him down. Talk to him. Convince him to take the job."

"Take the job?"

"You know. To . . . hack Kayla. Just take an arm or something. From the elbow down."

Percy looked like he'd eaten some bad scallops, his upper lip reaching for his nose. "I don't know."

"Come on, Purse. I've never asked you for a thing the entire time we've known each other. How many of your films have I helped you on?"

"Okay, this is different and you know it."

"I do know it. I know it's a big favor. Huge. But you don't have to do anything except help me research. Which is what you were doing anyway, right? Tracking this guy. Studying him?"

He threw his finger at me. "For no other reason than because I'm curious about how his mind works!"

"That's fair." I leaned back in my chair, somewhat enjoying the struggle Percy was having with this. If I'd been forced to wager, I would have put money on the notion Percy would have been totally down for this. His reaction came as quite the surprise. "But come on. Wouldn't it be cool to track down this psycho? Even if we don't find him? Wouldn't the detective work be . . . *fun*?"

He shuffled his feet, drank some beer. "Yeah, I guess."

"Good! Then you'll help me."

"I don't think I can do it."

"Come on."

"No, man. Kayla . . . Kayla is a nice girl. She doesn't deserve to have a limb hacked off."

My mood soured. A flutter of panic moved through me. After all this, all these hypotheticals and what-if scenarios, Percy was right. She didn't deserve that life, no matter how far we'd fallen for each other.

This was wrong.

Plain and simple.

Those disgusting images replayed, still shots of me hacking away at Kayla's numb corpse, and I instantly felt nauseous.

"You can't possibly do this to her . . . to someone you supposedly *love*."

I hung my head. Ashamed. I shouldn't have told Percy a goddamn thing. "You're right, Purse. This was nuts. I just . . . I love her, you know? I want to make it work. And I can't if she's . . . normal."

"I know, man. It sucks. But sometimes in life we have to make hard decisions, decisions that will crush us. But those things usually make us better. As humans. You'll come out of this on top. I promise."

"You think I should break it off with her? End this before it goes too far?"

But it had gone too far already—I knew that. These thoughts weren't the kind that would be easy to get rid of. These thoughts had roots, and they'd anchored themselves deep inside my psyche, refusing to let me go.

But still, I had gone too far, taken this to a level I didn't think I was capable of. And I knew this. Percy knew it too. He confirmed it with a curt nod. "I think you should get out of the grave before you dig yourself deeper."

I told him I'd do just that. I'd drop this whole Hacketstown Hacker plan and just move on. Break up with Kayla, revert back to my single life. Go back to trying to find someone I connect with who also fits my sexual fixation. There had to be someone else out there, someone *like* Kayla, someone smart and funny and who would be down for impromptu laser tag adventures, someone who'd laugh at all my bad jokes and watch terrible movies on the couch after a home-cooked meal. Someone who'd make my heart flutter every time I looked into her eyes. Yes, moving on was what I needed to do.

And so that was what I told Percy. *Ending things* was what I intended to do.

"I'm proud of you," he said, slapping my right shoulder.

We polished off the rest of the beers. I went home to call Kayla, planning to tell her the truth, the whole truth, weeding out every lie my damaged brain had produced over the last couple of weeks. I planned to come clean.

And to dump her.

FIFTEEN

IT'S easy to imagine everything you want to say, predict the things that will be said back to you, but it rarely plays out that way.

I called Kayla a quarter after ten, when I knew she'd be home from work. She answered the phone in that bubbly voice I'd grown very fond of. Just her simple inflections made me weak in the knees. Made my heart feel like someone had shaken a butterfly cage.

I didn't deserve her. She deserved someone who wouldn't lie to her, hide things. She deserved someone who wasn't considering lopping off a limb for their own selfish gratifications, their own sick fantasies.

"Hey there, lover," she said. "What's going on?"

I felt ill again. All the words I had practiced, recited in my head over and over again, were suddenly gone. My brain felt like a blank canvas. A bank account with no dollars. I couldn't withdraw the things I needed to say.

"Ray? You there?"

"Yeah, here."

"You okay? You sound . . . *off*."

"No, I'm good. Great, even." Another lie. Each one felt like a dagger digging beneath my skin, slicing me open. I knew this wouldn't end well. It couldn't; it was the nature of such things. Breakups were bad and there was no such thing as a good one, I don't care what anyone says. On some level, they're all messy.

"You don't sound great," she said, and I could tell she was smiling on the other end, but also leery of my tone. "You sound like maybe your dog died or something. Did your dog die? Do you even have a dog?"

"You know I don't have a dog."

"Then what's the deal-e-o?"

I breathed in, deep, and the air stabbed my lungs, a hundred spikes plunging into my chest. I couldn't intake a full breath. My heart jackhammered away. My vision was off, almost sideways. Sliding. The world rolled. Grew blurry. I'd never experienced a heart attack and couldn't even imagine what that would feel like, but what was happening to my body must have been pretty close. An elephant sat on my chest, squeezing everything inside.

"I . . . I have something to tell you."

Silence hung on her end. In the background, I heard the news. The anchor was talking about the Hacketstown Hacker, how he'd nabbed himself another victim, the second one this week. A woman had been found left on the side of the road, both arms severed at the shoulder, both wounds stitched to near perfection. *"A professional job,"* the anchor had said, *"which leads police to suspect the Hacker may be a surgeon or someone with an advanced medical background."* I wanted to get out what I needed to say, but I was too distracted by the news to continue. They went on to say how the Hacker was entering the stage of his career where serial killers often get sloppy, where their killings become more frequent. Less calculated. Where they make mistakes and get caught. Though the Hacker wasn't your traditional serial killer, he followed similar patterns. They were still labeling him as such.

"Ray?" Kayla said, snapping me out of it. "Ray, what's going on?" She sounded concerned now. Panicked. She sounded how I felt.

"I think we shouldn't see each other anymore," I blurted out, and hadn't meant to. Well, I did, but not like that. The direct approach was not what I was shooting for. There were lines I had rehearsed, certain things I needed to say. But in the end, they had become lost in my muddled mind, drowned beneath a sea of grotesque visions, horrid images of me taking a hatchet to one of my girlfriend's arms, a geyser of blood shooting out from the fresh wound like a busted faucet.

"What?" she said, gut-punched. Breathless.

"I'm sorry. I meant to explain everything first–"

"I don't understand, I thought–"

"Meant to tell you how I was feeling, but–"

"Thought things were going great and I really–"

"There are things I can't tell you–"

"My parents wanted to meet you and–"

We talked over each other for a solid thirty seconds.

"I'm sorry," I said finally, once the unpleasant silence had found us. "I wish there was something I could do."

"Do about what?" She was crying now. Oh, God, she was *crying*. And not a whimper or the cracked voice kind of crying, but full-on sobs now. "How's about not fucking break up with me? I thought things were going so well. We had a bunch of nice dates. The sex was great. Except, you know, for that first time, but once we got past that . . . amazing. And I . . . I . . . *I was falling in love with you.*"

That hit like a torpedo. We hadn't actually told each other how we felt about one another. I'd already fallen for her, fallen hard, but I hadn't the guts to utter those three fateful words. *I love you* was just something I had kept for myself and didn't plan to share until the time was absolutely perfect.

And now that time would never come.

"I'm sorry, I don't know what to do."

"How's about providing me with some explanation? Something that makes sense."

Oh, yeah, I thought, *so here's the thing, turns out you decided to date a guy who likes to have sex with amputees. Can't get it up with anyone else, which explains the first time we tried to do it. So, I've been taking little blue pills to prevent you from finding out until I figured out a long-term solution, which–get this–involved me cutting off one of your arms and legs, ruining your life forever. But hey! At least we could be happy, am I right?*

"I wish I could, but I can't."

She blew an exasperated sigh into my ear. "You can't. You can't? Ray, this doesn't make any sense. We've had two wonderful weeks together and—" She stopped herself. I heard her stifle some sobs. "You know what? It's not worth it."

"God, I'm sorry, Kay. I wish I could make this right."

"Is this a work thing? Is that it?"

"It's definitely not a work thing."

"Then what?"

"It's . . ." *I want to cut your fucking arms off!* "It's nothing. It's . . . I have a lot going on right now and—"

"What do you have going on? You live in a small apartment on the other side of town. You work at Best Tronics forty hours a week. You don't go to school. You don't have a lot of friends. You don't *do* anything except hang out with me or sleep or play video games or watch movies. So what is it? WHAT IS GOING ON?"

"I can't."

"Is it someone else? Oh God, it's someone else, isn't it. You've . . . you've met someone else."

"There's no one else." I felt tears sting my eyes. A second later, droplets began to leap down my cheeks and run along my jawline. "I'm just . . . not in the right state of mind."

"You know what? You don't want to tell me? Fine. Don't. Be that way."

She hung up.

I clutched my phone against my chest.

For a long while, I sat there. Frozen. Crying.

"Dude," Percy said the second I entered the break room the morning after last night's drama. "What did you say to Kayla?"

My heart thudded. The first thought I had was, *Oh Christ, she killed herself.*

"What happened?"

"She quit, man."

"Really?"

"Yeah. Gave Glen her notice this morning. What the fuck happened? Did you tell her, you know. . ." He ran his finger along his rotator cuff as if he were cutting his arm off. "Your secret?"

"No, of course not."

"Why the fuck not?"

"Because you know why. I didn't even want to tell *you.*"

"She probably thinks you're a complete asshole now."

"I am a complete asshole, Purse."

"Well . . . yeah . . . but now you're a complete asshole she wants nothing to do with."

"What was the alternative? Tell her about my problem, that I'm an amputee fucker, and let her believe I'm this huge freak, then have her break up with me anyway?" I shook my head. "No, it's better this way."

"Is it?"

I wondered: *Was it?*

"Yeah, I think it is."

Percy shook his head. "You should have told her the truth, man. I thought that's what we agreed on."

"We didn't agree on anything. We agreed I should call it quits with her because I started to have the craziest fucking thoughts in the world. Like, disturbing thoughts, Purse. And you agreed they were disturbing. And if you agreed they were disturbing, then I know they *were really fucking messed up,* man."

"Okay, okay. I get it. But still . . . she's going to paint you as an asshole to every girl that works here."

"Am I supposed to care?"

"I don't know. I would."

I didn't think Kayla would do that, talk about our issues with other female employees, but then again she was hurt and sometimes people do things out of character when they're hurting.

I was hurting.

I hurt badly. And I had considered things that were way out of character. I had thoughts that were so out of character I couldn't sleep at night. Yes, pain changes us. Makes us see the world differently. Pain, the psychological kind, can turn us crazy.

"All I know is last night I slept like a baby. No dreams. No nightmares of me sawing through one of Kayla's arms. Nothing of the sort."

"Well, good for you. As long as your conscience is clean."

"I don't know why you're so agitated. I did the right thing here."

"You should have told her. You owe her the truth. That's the right thing."

"Agree to disagree."

He shook his head and walked away.

I had nothing left to say anyway. So I punched in and went to work.

Went about my routines until Glen called me into the office about a half hour later.

This was apt to be a bad day.

"Everything okay?" Glen asked, peering at me over his glasses.

I was hardly paying attention. My eyes scanned the walls, glancing over his achievements and accolades. Framed certificates decorated the walls, documents of his college education and the various training classes he'd taken since joining Best Tronics. There were more than I remembered, not that I'd spent a lot of time in his office over the last three years. On the bookshelf behind him, trophies were lined up like soldiers holding the frontline.

"Ray?" he asked, pulling me out of a daydream. I'd slept great the night before, no dreams of ripping off Kayla's limbs, but as the day progressed, I found my mind wandering into darker territories. "Ray, are you listening to me?"

"Yeah, I'm here."

"Are you?"

"Yes."

"Normally I wouldn't dare pry into an employee's personal life, the company handbook forbids it, but when it affects the workplace, I'm instructed to inquire further."

"I understand."

"So, would you like to tell me the nature of your relationship with one of our newest employees, Kayla Marlowe?"

"We were . . . seeing each other."

"Dating?"

"Yeah."

"I see. And did something happen recently?"

"Glen, you know what happened."

"For the report," he said, pointing at the paperwork in front of him.

"Jesus, there's a report?"

"We just like to have documentation on these sorts of things. Strictly procedural."

I quickly got the sense this had nothing to do with Best Tronics. Why the fuck would corporate give a shit about two employees dating each other? Two regular associates nonetheless. It wasn't like I was a manager and she was my subordinate. I had seniority over her, sure, but it wasn't like we violated a major work rule. Or a minor one. It didn't add up. I wondered if this was for nothing more than Glen's own amusement.

Always knew he was a big weirdo. Probably got off on other people's problems.

"Nothing *happened,* Glen. We were dating and now we're not. End of fucking story."

He pursed his lips. "What have I told you about language in the workplace, even if it's off the floor?"

"Sorry, but I find this a little ridiculous."

"I told you. Strictly–"

"Yeah, so if I call corporate right now, that's the answer they'll give me?"

His eyes were on me like lasers, burning into my flesh. "Go ahead." He picked up the phone and offered it to me. "I'll dial the number for you."

I was tempted but ultimately declined. I wanted to be out of the office, far away from Glen and his smelly breath and his stupid plaques noting all his stupid accomplishments. The less time I spent in there the better. I was beginning to feel claustrophobic. The walls were closing in, squishing me. I felt flattened.

"Now," he said, putting the phone back down on the cradle. "Tell me."

"Honestly, it's no big deal. We were dating, and I decided to break things off."

"Why?"

"Because I wasn't feeling it, man. Okay?"

"Fine. It's just weird she up and gave her notice like that."

"What are you implying?"

"Nothing, nothing. Just wanted to make sure there wasn't . . . anything else."

"There's nothing else."

"Okay." He put his hands up in surrender. "Okay. Just, if something comes out later that you didn't admit now, it might look bad. That's all."

I wasn't sure what he wanted me to say. But what I had told him was close enough to the truth and I planned on leaving it at that.

I pushed myself up from the desk. "Are we done, then?"

"Yes." He closed the report. "Go back to work. Help Sadie stock out the cell phone shipment."

I left the office and closed the door. I could've sworn I heard Glen say, *"And try not to fuck her either,"* after the door was shut, but I couldn't be sure. I might have imagined he said that, my mind further proving its god-like strength.

Asshole, I thought as I headed to the floor, thinking all I needed was a little work to keep myself busy and to keep my mind off Kayla.

To keep my mind off going to those dark places.

Places where I held a bloody knife and a clean rag, wearing a sick, twisted smile on my face while Kayla screamed.

Screamed for me to help her. Screamed while I cut into her flesh and muscle and bone.

SIXTEEN

THE next few days were rough. I spent a lot of time with myself, which was bad, because that also meant I spent a lot of time with my thoughts. I thought breaking it off with Kayla would be a good thing, that it would help—for the first day or two, it did. But then my thoughts turned on me like a bad drug. The images that came to me during the day were more visceral. And growing increasingly frequent. While we were dating, the images popped up maybe once or twice a day, leaving me almost as quickly as they had come. But now, they were hitting me almost every other hour. Graphic scenes of me swinging a mallet against her shoulder, over and over again until her arm was nothing but a limp, fleshy sock of shattered bones. Then I would take scissors to her thin skin and cut away. My brain conjured only the most difficult ways to sever an arm or a leg, like, they rarely depicted me hacking through the bone with a handsaw. Another image had me stringing her up like a piñata, beating her limbs with a baseball bat until they came undone and candy fell out. I'd greedily gather the candy and start feeding myself with it, like a starved animal who had just stumbled out of hibernation.

I couldn't take it anymore. I thought about seeing someone, a professional, hoping maybe they could give me some medication to make the images go away. To make the night terrors stop. Something that would keep me from waking up in a lake of cold sweat with a head full of bad dreams.

But I couldn't bring myself to go through with it. I had actually gone as far as to make the appointment, but I bailed fifteen minutes prior to the scheduled time. I got super nervous, thinking if I confided in this man or woman everything that was happening inside my head, they'd send me straight to the insane asylum. Lock me up with no key. Of course, I considered doctor/patient confidentiality, but I think that shit goes out the window when you admit to having lucid thoughts of you hacking another human being to pieces. Pretty sure there's a line and that crosses it.

Speaking of crosses, here I was—at a *cross*road. I couldn't live with these images in my head. I couldn't live with only two hours of uninterrupted sleep. I couldn't live knowing the love of my life was out there, hurting because of something I did to her—knowing I couldn't be honest with her and tell her anything. Sure, now that we weren't together, I guess I could have told her the truth. Maybe she'd even want me back. Maybe she cared enough to forgive my lies and deceit, maybe she'd even care enough to help me through this little dilemma. I mean, I doubted she'd offer up an arm or a leg, but maybe she'd help seek out an answer. Maybe with her support, a doctor wouldn't be so apt to throw me in the looney bin.

But I couldn't do that. What if she didn't react that way? What if she thought I was a total freak? What if she *did* tell everyone my secrets? About my fixation on female amputees. I couldn't have that. I'd have to quit, move to another town. Hell, maybe even another state. And I didn't want to do that—I liked it here. Wasn't much of one, but I *had* made a life here.

I thought about killing myself. Just for a second. I'm not proud of it. But in those moments of personal torment, especially when I looked at Kayla to see what I'd done to her, what I'd made her into, I didn't think there was any other way out. I thought the only way to end it was to *end it*. End everything.

But I didn't want to do that either. Like I said, I liked it here. I enjoyed living. Even if it wasn't the most glamorous lifestyle—I got by. I made enough money where I ate well every day, could afford rent, cable, and Internet, plus a little extra spending money per week. Some weeks were tighter than others, but I never starved.

Anyway, my life was pretty good.

I wanted to keep living. And I wanted to keep living with Kayla there, next to me, by my side, through thick and thin.

I needed to fix this.

And the only thing I kept coming back to was my thoughts, the ones that feasted on my positive vibes; the ones that had ground me down. Chewed me up like a stick of jerky.

I finally decided maybe there was a way I *could* have everything. That I could have it all. And that was to follow the thoughts. To give into them.

I couldn't do it myself; I had already decided that.

But maybe someone else could. Someone with experience. Someone who was already doing it.

The Hacketstown Hacker.

Yes, I thought I should find him. Convince him. Present to him his next victim.

Then I could have it all.

The perfect life. Everything I'd always wanted.

But would I feel guilty? Yes, of course. But I'd have to learn to live with it. Maybe the guilt wouldn't project gruesome images into my brain, wouldn't keep me up at night, leaving me to bathe in puddles of my own perspiration.

Maybe.

Then again, maybe they still would.

SEVENTEEN

I hung around the cluster of bushes near the exit ramp, partially hiding myself from interested eyes, waiting for the meeting to break. Beside me, some dude blew smoke into the frigid atmosphere. His breath ghosted into the chilly night. He pulled on his cigarette several more times, clouds shrouding much of the surrounding area. I didn't think he saw me, and if he did, I didn't care. I was here for one reason and one reason only—to make a friend.

Or to win back a friend.

The meeting broke and a small group paraded down the exit ramp. I emerged from my semi-hidden position when I saw her face.

"Don't scream," I said, putting my hands up like an offensive lineman ready to throw a block. "I just need to talk to you."

Wendy stood there, frozen, staring at me, her eyes as icy as the walkway. She was about two seconds away from exploding. I could see her face turn several shades of crimson and it wasn't due to the frigid gusts of winter winds.

I was done for.

Coming here had been a dumb idea.

But as the seconds came off the clock, I realized she wasn't going to do that, she wasn't going to blow up my spot.

"What the hell do you want?" she asked, sounding as if she were biting her tongue.

"Just to talk. Over coffee. There's a nice diner around the corner. My treat?"

"Hey, Wendy!" some guy called over. He and his friend were smoking on the other side of the walkway. His prosthetic hand held his cigarette while he puffed fog into the air. "This guy bothering you?"

She hesitated. For a second, I thought she'd give me up. Expose me for the monster I was. Then: "No, he's fine. Just an old friend."

Surprised no one else recognized me, but then again I'd only come to this meeting once. If they had, no one said anything. The rest of the group lingered at the end of the ramp, smoking and talking and laughing, commenting on the weather and how damn cold it was, trying to figure out a place they could all go and hang out, somewhere warm.

"You look good," I said, commenting on her new prosthetic.

She looked down at it, stared as if reflecting upon how it came to be a part of her. Her eyes lingered there, and I cleared my throat to help speed things up. It was cold—*so fucking cold*—and I couldn't ignore the every-three-second casual glances people were throwing us.

"Thanks," she said.

"So, look, I *really* need to talk to you. Diner? Please?"

She didn't look like she wanted to.

"I'll beg if you want?"

She shook her head. "Your treat?"

"Of course."

"This isn't some sleazy attempt to fuck me again?"

"Absolutely not."

"Promise?"

"Swear my life on it."

The coffee came quickly and thank goodness for that. Despite the steam rising from the black surface, I drank a few sips anyway, embracing the burn. I felt like I was about to get burned anyway—

where this conversation was headed I had no idea, but it wasn't trending toward a positive ending.

"Excuse me?" she asked, her jaw dropping open. Staying there.

"I saw your name in the paper. I know you didn't lose that arm in a car accident."

She tucked her arms close to her, her real one falling over the prosthetic, then looked away, concentrating hard on the first thing she laid eyes on. If I were writing a book about this conversation, I'd write something like "and her face blanched at the realization she'd been caught." Or something like that. I don't know. I've never actually seen someone's face blanch before, but she looked all sorts of sickly. Disgusted. Done with this conversation before it ever began.

Above all else, getting caught had made her uncomfortable. She shifted around in the booth, her pants rubbing against the leather sounding off like funny fart noises. It was hard for her to sit still after that.

After I burned my mouth a few more times, she finally faced me.

"Look, I don't want anyone to know, okay?"

I felt my brow climb my forehead. "Well now we each have a secret to keep." I paused, seeing if her expression would change, but it didn't. "May I ask why?"

For a second, I didn't think she'd answer. Then: "Embarrassed."

"It's nothing to be embarrassed about."

She nearly growled. "What would you know about it?"

A valid question; one I didn't have an immediate response for. "Nothing. Absolutely nothing."

"Then how can you tell me how to feel?"

"I guess . . . I guess I can't."

She nodded, knowing she'd won that battle.

"Look, Wendy. I'm sorry. I didn't come here to call you out on a lie, make you feel bad, or anything like that."

"What did you bring me here for?"

"I want your help."

"With?"

"With finding him."

"Finding him?"

"Yeah. . ." My finger drew invisible circles on the tabletop. "Yeah . . . I want to find him."

"Why?"

"To stop him, I guess." The lies were coming pretty easily, which, in turn, made *me* uncomfortable.

"You want to stop him?" I could see tears building in her eyes, threatening to fall. Wetness swelled near the rims.

"Yeah, I think he's bad and he does bad things and I think he should be stopped."

"What makes you think you can track him down better than the police?"

"Solid question. I, uh, am more motivated to."

"More motivated?"

"Yeah, I think we're getting sidetracked here. I'm supposed to be interviewing *you.* Not the other way around."

She sat back, folded her arm across her body. "I think you're full of shit."

"Maybe I am."

"Does this have something to do with your weird, sexual . . . I don't even know what you'd call it."

"Some things are better left unlabeled." Sipped more coffee. Put my elbows on the table and leaned forward. I was getting tired of this song and dance. I needed some answers. "I want to ask you about the Hacketstown Hacker. What you remember from the incident. Please. I know you don't owe me shit, I know I have no right to ask, but please. I . . . I need to know what you know."

Staring at me for a long time, she searched my face, waiting for me to give up the truth. But having had a lot of practice, I'd become good at concealing the truth. My face was a mask of no expression. I returned her gaze, twice as stony.

"Okay," she said, freeing her real arm. She tapped the table with her nails, breaking up the silence and delaying the conversation. "What is it you want to know?"

"Do you have any idea who he is? What he looks like?"

She shook her head. Tears continued to stand on the rims of her eyes, their descent inevitable. "No. I told some detectives what I remember. Which isn't much. I was drugged for most of it."

"How did he . . . take you?"

She opened her mouth, but her lips only spread so far. Something kept them from opening all the way, allowing her to speak. I assumed that was fear, the same fear that strangled her vocal cords. Hesitating, she squinted as if the details were still fuzzy, unclear. Finally, words broke through. "It's honestly hard for me to remember. I recall doing things that day. I remember going to work that morning, food shopping after, heading to the gym. The last thing I can clearly remember is the gym. Took a Zumba class that night. But they have cameras inside and in the parking lot, and they showed me driving away. So it couldn't have happened there." She paused, drank some coffee—a big gulp—then resumed. "They don't know what happened after that. I was found in my car three days later, parked on the side of the highway. He only took an arm . . ." She sniffled. I could tell this was hurting, having to relive these moments. *Why put her through this? What would she tell me that would help crack the case?* I started to feel bad about bringing her here. Making her revisit this obviously traumatic event. But maybe there was something, something that would prove worth it. A little hint that would jar something loose. Break this mystery wide open. Probably not, but Wendy was the best shot I had. "He only took an arm, and the police told me the surgery was done by a near professional."

"Near? The news suggested the man was a surgeon or something."

"A doctor confirmed that, although everything seemed done by the book, there was way too much bruising. 'Done without grace,' was what they told me. A real doctor would have been more careful. Also might have had access to more state-of-the-art equipment, by the way, the police said the hack job could have been done with gardening tools from Home Depot. So . . . who knows for sure." She wiped her nose with her finger. A tear leaked down the side of her face.

"I'm so sorry that happened."

She cried a little. I handed her a napkin, which she immediately used to blot the falling tears.

"It's funny," she said, blowing her nose. "I thought you were him."

"Me?" I chuckled, finding the idea funny. More than funny. Ludicrous. Fucking bonkers. But she wasn't joking. "Me?" I said again, incredulously this time.

"Yeah, *you.* After that day in the supermarket. I thought maybe you were running around the state, hacking girls' arms and legs off to satisfy your sick obsession."

That actually made a lot of sense, hearing it aloud.

"Almost called the detectives who interviewed me. The ones that gave me their cards and told me to call them if I ever *remembered* anything else."

"And why didn't you?"

She looked at me, *really* looked at me. Through me. Inside me. Infiltrated my brain, rummaged around my thoughts. "Because. I remember pieces."

"Pieces?"

"Of being in his presence. Little flashes. I don't remember the details, not from the neck up. He had it hidden the whole time anyway, behind a surgical mask and a powder-blue hairnet."

"And?"

"He was bigger than you. Taller. A little less scrawny. Not as bony. It was someone who took care of himself. Someone who prided himself on his appearance."

I was a little hurt by the scrawny-bony bit, but I let it go.

"Did he speak?"

She nodded. "Oh, yes. He spoke."

"What did he say?"

"Mostly how I'd become one of his angels. He was God and he'd make a whole army of angels to worship him. Weird stuff like that. I suppose that could've been the drugs, too. Maybe I was hallucinating. Maybe I just imagined him saying those things."

"I guess it's possible."

"Anyway, the guy's voice didn't match yours. Though, I was high and he could have sounded like anyone. Maybe my memories are fucking with me. Maybe what I remember isn't even real."

Our food came. We dug in. I ate my omelet in record time.

"Anything else you can give me?" I asked, after the last bite was in my mouth.

She continued to sample her pancakes and the different syrups the diner had to offer. "No, nothing. It all feels like a bad dream. The last thing I remember is waking up in my car, groggy from a head full of painkillers. Though, they didn't do much. My shoulder felt like someone dropped a boulder on it."

"Goddamn, I'm so sorry that happened to you."

"Are you?"

I was taken aback. "Of course. Why wouldn't I be?"

"This guy has what . . . six victims?"

"I think he's up to eight now. The last news report I saw said he might have two more. Two girls went missing after a Hacketstown High football game. They can't be sure it's him, but . . . they're treating it as such."

"He'll never stop."

"He's getting reckless. They say, anyway."

She stuffed her mouth full of pancakes topped with blueberry syrup, but that didn't prevent her from responding. "Anyway, my point is, this guy is running around, taking people's arms and legs off, right? And not people, but *women."*

"What's your point?"

"My point is, *Ray,* is this psycho is doing your dirty work."

"My dirty work? What the–"

"He's creating the very objects you desire."

"Whoa, whoa. Women are not objects, okay? That's not how I view them. That's not how I view this whole . . . *situation* at all."

"Isn't it, though?"

"I'm not some shallow asshole, okay? I take into account the people I sleep with's feelings, okay?"

"You keep telling yourself that, but I don't think it's true." She sliced herself another forkful. "You tell yourself you do it because you want to 'emotionally connect' with someone, you want the sex to be meaningful, but let's face it . . . these women you're bringing to bed with you, they're nothing more than a sock you'd jerk off into."

"That's not true and you know it."

She sat back and folded her arm again. Her eyes had dried up, and now a slick smile had conquered the lower half of her face. It was as if she'd won something. In a way, maybe she had. "I think it is, Ray. I think a guy like you isn't capable of loving anyone. This acrotomo-whatever you call it . . . it's just an excuse to bed women when they're at their lowest low."

"Not true. At all."

"Face it. You're scum."

"I'm not . . ." I almost told her *I'm not a monster.* "I have a girlfriend right now, actually. A girl I'm in love with."

"Oh," she said, pretending this news had surprised her. "Oh, a girlfriend, *Ray.* You have a girlfriend?"

"Your sarcasm isn't necessary, *Wendy."* I was getting pissed. She could tell. It pleased her. I guess I deserved the abuse for the lies I told her, the untruths I used in order to get her in the sack. "But yes, I have a girlfriend and we're . . . very happy together. In fact, I think she might be *the one."*

"That's beautiful, Ray. And hey, does she know about your little . . . let's call it a sickness, because that's what it is, isn't it? A sickness? A disease that's plaguing you. Plaguing the rest of us too, if you think about it."

"It's not a sickness. It's just a . . . preference."

"You told me you're only attracted to amputees. I'm guessing that means you can't get it up with anyone else. Am I correct to assume that?"

I didn't answer but I let my eyes exude the truth.

"That's what I thought. I think that makes it a sickness. You're a fucking headcase, Ray."

"Call it what you want. I know who I am."

"Do you?"

I shook my head in disbelief. This was not how I pictured our meal would go. But I had gotten what I needed from her. I had gotten her take on the events that happened to her, that led us down this path. I could have thrown down thirty bucks on the table and bounced anytime I wanted to.

"Yes, I do."

"Well, good for you, Ray. Good for fucking you."

"I've been nothing but nice to you. Treated you with respect."

She broke on this note. Covering her face with her hands, she sobbed heavily into her palms. Surrounding patrons immediately took notice, craning their heads in our direction. People on the other side of the diner rose from their seats, peeking over the booths to have a better look at the drama unfolding. *Vultures. Social vultures.* Our waitress made for our table and I waved her off, giving her the international sign for *everything's all right, we're just gonna need a moment.*

"I know you're hurting. But you'll be all right. You'll get through this. I'm sorry I brought you here. I thought . . . I dunno. I thought talking about this stuff might help you in some way."

"You want to help?" she asked through her fingers.

"Yeah, honestly, I do." That wasn't a lie–not completely. Wendy was awesome; I saw traces of just how cool of a human being she could be on the night we slept together. But her tragedy had taken a lot of her spirit away. Now she was in the business of blaming, trying to drag everyone around her down with her. It was a common practice I'd seen many times before or had heard about while attending meetings. I wanted to help Wendy. I wanted to make things right. I wanted to free her from the pain keeping her down.

I am not a monster.

"You can find him," she said, lowering her hands. "You can find him and make him pay in a way the police can't."

"I'll do my best."

"Kill him. For me. For all the women out there like me. That's how you can make this right."

"I . . . I don't think I can kill him, I just want to–"

"Kill him," she growled. Her mascara had bled black streaks down her face. Her lips trembled with fury, the hatred she'd stored over the last several months finally exploding outward. Her teeth clenched, so tightly I thought they might break off at the root. *"Kill him."*

Then her features went soft. There was something cherubic about her now. Something that frightened me.

"For me," she said, her voice barely a whisper. "Please."

EIGHTEEN

IT was Kayla's last day, and she spent the entire morning changing price tags on the appliances and big-ticket items. I tried several times to waltz over there and say something to her, something that would make up for the bullshit I had dragged her through.

Something that would make up for her broken heart.

I wanted to tell her I would find a way to fix us, but there was no way I could do so without explaining everything. Maybe Percy had been right: the truth was the way to go. Didn't some scholarly mind, some philosopher once say, "The truth will set you free." It was probably true, the truth *would* set me free. Free from everything I kept hidden deep inside my skull, kept buried in a dark place. But I didn't want to do that because the truth was also a dagger. A dagger that was heading straight for the center of my chest.

The truth was death.

Kayla was life.

I needed to live.

About the fourth time I passed by the appliances, Kayla noticed me. Our eyes connected for a few seconds—which felt like an eternity—and I was the first to look away. The sixth time I sauntered by, she stopped me.

"Hey!" she said, approaching me.

I stopped, but didn't turn toward her. I didn't want my eyes to settle on her for too long–I figured that would spark my brain to project those awful images again. The scenes of me slashing off an arm or a leg, the ones that made me puke.

I tested myself and allowed my vision to find her, stay with her. My imagination cooperated, and no such violent scenarios played out between my ears.

"Hey," I said weakly.

"So, this is my last day. Not sure if you knew or not."

"Yeah, I heard." I turned and faced her, but not before peeking around the store, seeing if anyone was watching us. No one was–the shoppers were busy shopping and the workers were all hiding from customers or running around, completing their daily tasks. "Kayla, I wish I could fix this thing."

"What thing is that?"

"Me."

"What's wrong with you?" She was tranquil, sounding at peace. On the outside. On the inside I could tell she was still hurting. A lot.

I almost told her then, in the middle of the goddamn store. *I'm a sick freak with a strange sexual fixation and my dick is broken.* Almost. The words were right there, on the tip of my tongue–I couldn't pull the trigger. Hell, I even opened my mouth to speak those exact words. In the end, I had failed to fire.

"I dunno. Lots of things, probably."

"I'm afraid I'll need a better explanation than that."

"Look, don't quit. I know it sucks and it's been awkward, but don't quit because of me."

Her eyes darted around the store. "It's too late."

"It's not too late. You can march back to the office and tell Glen you rescind your notice. I've seen people do it before."

Looking down at the ground, she said, "I don't think you understand . . ."

"What?"

"It's hard to look at you, Raymond." Off her lips, my full name didn't sound so good anymore. She shook her head, then brushed away a wisp of blonde hair that had fallen in front of her eyes. "I don't think you know how much I'd fallen for you."

That hit like a punch in the gut. "I fell for you too."

"Then why the fuck did you end things with me?"

"It wasn't supposed to be this way."

"What the fuck does that even mean?" She balled her fists and shook them at me, grunted with frustration. "Do you know how frustrating this is? I know you're hiding something from me, and I don't know what it is, but sooner or later I *will* find out. Whatever it is, I'll find out."

I didn't care for her tone, the threatening nature of it, but I guess it was what I deserved. She had earned herself the truth, but I was too much of a coward to share it. The weird part was I knew she could handle it. Hell, a larger part of me knew she'd accept me no matter what. That she'd work with me, assist me through whatever troubles I may have had. But I'd lived with the secret so damn long that it was *my* secret. I didn't want to share it, at least not with her. I felt dirty inside, stained, inadequate. Even if she "accepted" me, there was a part of me that would always suspect she'd think of me as inferior. A lesser human being. Something that was broken, something that constantly needed fixing and maintenance. A quest for her to conquer. Just a chore.

Right or wrong, those were my feelings. I couldn't control them, rein them in. Just like I couldn't find myself attracted to women with all their limbs attached.

"I'm sorry, Kayla. I never wanted to hurt you. I just . . ."

"What?" she said, her eyes begging for the truth. She even grabbed my hand, interlaced our fingers. This was not the kind of conversation to be held on the sales floor, and if Glen happened to pass by, he'd be super pissed. But I didn't give a shit who saw us. Her touch was the best thing I'd felt in weeks. "What is it?"

"I just need to sort a few things out."

"What things?"

"Personal things."

"What kind of *personal* things?"

"If I told you, then it wouldn't be personal anymore."

"You can tell me anything. You know that, don't you?"

I nodded. "Please. I'll fix this. I'll fix me." I shook my head. Tears squeezed their way out from the corners of my eyes. "But don't quit. It will be okay."

"I'm embarrassed. The whole store knows you broke up with me."

"I know, but . . . shit. If that's what you're worried about, we can tell them you broke up with me."

She shook her head. "No, I don't care what they think. It's just . . . awkward working here now. I can work practically anywhere for a dollar above minimum wage."

"If that's how you feel. But I wish you'd reconsider. I like . . . I *enjoy* seeing your face when I come to work."

Water immediately spilled over the rims of her eyes, flushed down her face. "Excuse me," she said, then let go of my hands and stormed off, heading toward the restroom.

I didn't follow.

I watched her go, thinking that would be the last time I'd ever see her.

I tried one last time to fix this on my own. I decided to see someone. A shrink. A head doctor. Maybe he could psychoanalyze me, tell me what I needed to do to correct my *situation,* and it was a situation now. Not just a lifestyle choice or some sexual preference. Hearts were involved–it was a *fucking situation.*

It was a few days after Kayla's last day. Someone told me she had already gotten a new job in the mall at one of those centrally located stands, the ones that sell dumb stuff like cheap-ass drones and anklet charms. I didn't know which one, but I could have easily found out by going there. Anyway, I had an appointment downtown and I arrived at Dr. Bennet's office fifteen minutes early so I could fill out the packet of paperwork most doctors require on the initial visit.

Twenty minutes after that, I was sitting down on a very comfortable black couch. Dr. Bennet came in five minutes after that. He was a scholarly-looking dude, sporting a full beard, gray-brown with streaks of white throughout. He wore glasses that were pushed all the way up his nose and much too close to his face. His hair was short, also a brownish gray and peppered with patches of pure white. He flashed me a smile and shook my hand, introduced himself.

"So what brings you in today?" he asked, flipping the hourglass upside down on his desk and sitting down. His office chair looked like it cost more than my rent.

The hourglass, I thought, was a nice touch.

"Oh boy, where do I begin?"

"It's usually best to begin at the beginning," he said humorously, which I liked. I needed it. I needed to smile. It felt weird to smile in this environment, almost wrong, but it also felt kinda good, like *really* fucking good.

"Do you know what acrotomophilia is?"

His eyes narrowed at the mention of my affliction. My torment. My own personal hell.

"That, I believe, is the term used for those who enjoy sexual encounters with amputees." He spouted this off as if he were unsure, but I could tell he knew exactly what he was talking about. "Is that what you're referring to?"

"Precisely."

"And, it's why you're here today?"

"It is."

"Tell me about it."

I told him about it. Everything. Everything from the time I saw an attractive woman in the mall with no arms, how that sparked my fascination. From then on I explained my formative years, what you might call *coming-of-age*. High school, my awkwardness around the opposite sex. How I didn't have sex until I was twenty-two, with a woman I'd pulled off some sleazy website that mingled amputees. A slight mental breakdown at twenty-four, that quick stay at a mental health facility an hour north because I'd attempted to cut my wrists in the bathtub and thank God my mother had found me in time, told me her *intuition* told her I was in trouble. Weren't for that, I might have gone through with it. Good times. All of it. I felt uncomfortable traveling back to these places, but at the same time, it felt good to get it all out there.

"So, your sexual fantasies regarding amputees . . . you view this as a problem?" asked Bennet, clicking the top of his pen.

"Isn't it?"

"People have different tastes, Mr. Bridges. As long as it harms no one, I'd say it's purely a preference, even if it is outside the norm."

"See that's the problem. I want to be normal."

"Have you tried with someone who isn't—"

"Oh yeah." I went and told him everything about Kayla. Made sure to tell him how much I loved her, how much I cared about her, how much I needed to flip this situation on its head. And fast. Before I lost her. "So, you see, I need to . . . you know . . . find her attractive."

"Well, I'm afraid that's a little more complicated. The Viagra seems to work for you, though. I recommend sticking with it."

"That's just a Band-aid over the real problem. The real problem being I don't find the girl I've fallen for, connected with on a level I never have in my entire, shitty life, particularly attractive in the physical sense."

"Quite a dilemma, I must say."

"So can you help me or no?"

"Mr. Bridges," he said. He was smiling. I didn't care for it now, now that we were getting into it. "The brain is a powerful tool. It can't simply be 'rewired.' There are some deep, psychological aspects to this that can't simply be treated with a pill or a prescription. To put this simply, you can't be *fixed.* And a part of it is because you're not broken. Not really."

My face grew hot. A second later, my entire body felt on fire. I was mad, but it was an embarrassed kind of anger. I'd bled my soul in front of this guy, and he wasn't telling me anything other than what I already knew. I wasn't broken. I didn't need to be fixed.

I am not a monster.

"My suggestion, seriously, is to stick with the blue pills. In time, who knows, maybe you won't need them anymore."

"Really? That's the plan?"

"What did you expect? For me to hypnotize you? Say something like, 'Good news! When you wake up, you'll find *all* women sexually desirable, no matter how many limbs they have. Bad news; you'll quack like a duck every time someone says the word *shrink.*" He laughed, but I didn't. "Sorry, a little shrink humor."

I left after that, feeling no better than I had when I arrived. Actually, I felt worse.

And after all that, only one thought remained: *find him.*

Find the Hacketstown Hacker.

NINETEEN

GETTING your review at work is one of the worst experiences of the year. You've been there, we all have. No one would argue having your weaknesses pointed out and shoved in your face is about as much fun as having your nipples hooked up to a car battery, unless you're into nipple stuff, in which case you might like it. (I think that makes sense.) But I'm getting off track and talking about nipples, so let me stop myself and get back to the story at hand.

As Glen sat me down to beat me up over my yearly performance, he flashed me a smile. A knowing smile, a smile I immediately wanted to knock off the side of his face. The smile was almost predatory, like the way a lioness would regard a grazing gazelle. *I'm going to get you,* that smile said, and even though it was only a review, meaningless in the grand scheme of current affairs, I couldn't help but embrace the chill that ran across my arms, shoulders, and neck.

"So . . . how're things?" he asked.

"Fine. Great, even."

"Good. I'm glad. Couldn't help but notice you and Kayla over by the appliances last week."

Shit. This guy seemed to have the same power as Mark, the

store manager—he saw everything that happened in this place. He must have had eyes in the goddamn appliances. Everywhere, maybe. Eyes all over the fucking place. Did he watch security footage in his spare time? I pictured him downloading copies onto a portable disk drive and taking the content home with him, spending hours upon hours sifting through the day's mundane happenings—a little foreplay before he combed the web and jacked off to cosplay porn.

(Still firmly believe the last two sentences to be true.)

"Yeah, we were . . . talking."

"Mm-hm." He was still smiling, still proud. Of what, I was afraid to find out. "Well, whatever you said to her, it must have worked."

"Come again?"

"She came in yesterday, asking for her old job back."

"Really?" I guess I looked more shocked than happy. His smile stumbled a little.

"Yes, really. Said the other job wasn't treating her very well. Said she'd rather come back here."

"How very interesting."

"Indeed."

"Well? Did you hire her back?"

"Of course."

"Well . . . good."

"Is it?"

I sat back and let out a deep breath. This circle jerk of a conversation was getting us nowhere. "Do you have something you want to tell me, Glen?"

"Just wanted your opinion on it."

"Since when do you care about my opinion?" Okay, that sounded bad, but it was a knee-jerk reaction to his dumb questions and bush-beating. "Sorry, that came out wrong."

He didn't change his face. Still wearing that smile, he shuffled my review before him. "A good manager always takes his employees' opinions into account. You'd do well to remember that if you want to consider a future here. Or anywhere."

Well, if *considering employees' opinions* was the case, then Glen had failed as a manager in my first three years. I suddenly wondered if he'd had his own review recently, and this was the result of the store manager's—Mark Barr, the true eye in the sky—suggestions on how Glen could improve. I suspected so.

"It's fine with me. It would be great to have her back."

"There wouldn't be any . . . conflict?"

"Things didn't end on a good note, exactly, but we're professional. It won't interfere with work."

Satisfied, Glen nodded. "All right then. Onto your review."

He spent the next fifteen minutes telling me what I did right and wrong over the last twelve months, gave me tips on how to improve as a worker, how to possibly rise up the ranks and become an assistant store manager just like him. I didn't have the stones to tell him I'd rather eat horse shit every day for the rest of my life than become something like him. He blathered on for a few more minutes, but I drowned him out. My eyes were drawn to the walls, the framed certificates hanging there. The ones I'd seen before but never actually bothered to notice. My eyes had never lingered on them for more than a few seconds; never read the actual verbiage displayed so proudly.

They were impressive.

Turned out, Glen didn't go to any old community college—he went to the Perelman School of Medicine in Pennsylvania. Pretty prestigious, as I found out later. He had a dozen certificates and diplomas hanging there, out in view. For all to see. For anyone who stepped foot in the office. Like I had so many times and completely ignored.

My eyes found one in particular, one I couldn't look away from. It stated he'd completed five years of surgical residency at a local hospital.

A surgeon.

My stomach turned. The images of me standing over Kayla with a chainsaw in my hand, ready to chew through one of her arms was suddenly replaced by a similar image—Glen standing over her, a mad smile pinned to his face, echoes of a sinister cackle drifting between my ears.

"Are you listening, Ray?" he asked.

I nodded, but only once—further movement might have caused me to hurl all over the man's workspace.

"You okay?" he asked. "You look sick. You still eating a lot of sushi on your lunch breaks? How many times—"

"It's nothing. I'm fine." I tried to focus on his face, but every time I blinked, I saw bright red freckles of blood attached to his skin. I blinked and they went away. Blinked again and they were back.

"You sure?"

"Yeah." My eyes betrayed the situation, as he found me glancing back at his superfluous wall art.

He smiled, but it wasn't a proud display this time. "I know what you're thinking . . ."

My stomach dropped. I pictured him reaching under his desk, grabbing some tool perfectly designed for splitting open my flesh, and running it across the softest part of my neck.

". . . you probably want to know how I ended up here after all . . ."—he jerked his thumb toward the wall—". . . all that."

"That's," I said, barely able to breathe, "exactly what I was thinking."

He gave me a cautious look, then continued. "In the fifth year of my residency, I was tasked with saving a man's life. He'd been having chest pains and a CT scan revealed there may have been a blockage in his LAD—one of the main arteries leading to the heart. It's called the widowmaker because the mortality rate is much higher than other blocked arteries. Anyway, we went in. And. . ." I noticed his eyes took on a glassy reflection. "And I nicked the artery. It was bad. His chest started filling up with blood. He was dead before we could even attempt any kind of emergency rescue operation."

He stared past me, back into those days, however long ago they had been. I almost pitied him. He hadn't been the nicest manager, certainly not the best I'd ever worked for and certainly not the worst—but I can't say I liked him. He was too much of a corporate sock puppet for me to ever relate to. In that moment though, he'd shed his corporate skin and become entirely too human. Too real. A single teardrop fell from his lashes, splashing on the desk below.

"Sorry that happened to you," was all I could say.

He didn't respond. He kept staring, replaying the horrific event over and over again, a prisoner of that time and place. I shifted uncomfortably. My eyes fell elsewhere—the ground, the wall, the door—anywhere but his nearly lifeless stare.

Then he snapped out of it. "Sorry. Got lost back there." His smile returned, but it was hardly authentic. The smile was a Band-Aid for his pain. "Where was I?"

"Ummm. You were about to give me my raise and kick me out."

Nodding, he reached under the review and pulled out a list with every employee's yearly increase. He gave me the number (which wasn't all that much, but hey . . . a raise was a raise) and saw me to the door.

Shook my hand.

When I took back my hand, it was covered in scarlet.

Blood. My palm was filled with it.

I blinked and the blood was gone.

TWENTY

"YOU think *Glen* is the Hacketstown Hacker?" Percy asked, tossing his empty beer bottle in the recyclables next to his stepfather's workbench. "What the fuck, dude?"

"I know it sounds weird. Even impossible. But, dude, you should have seen him during my review." I told him about the certificates and diplomas, how I'd finally read and asked about them. "He freaked out."

"Like yelling?"

"No, not yelling." Percy sure was stupid sometimes. "Like, he almost had a mental breakdown. Got real somber. Apparently he killed a guy during his residency."

"What the fuck is a residency?"

"It's like paid training for doctors and surgeons. Anyway, he was going inside some guy—"

"—that just sounds weird—"

"—and he accidentally nicked an artery. Guy bled out instantly and died right before him."

"That's fucking dark, dude."

"Glen actually *killed* a guy."

"Guessing that's why he gave it all up and became a manager at Best Tronics."

"Yep. You should have seen his face. He was haunted, man. *Haunted.* Surprised he keeps that shit hanging there. I know if that happened to me, I'd never want to look at a diploma with my name on it. I'd bury that shit. Deep."

"Man. I never would have guessed."

"It all adds up, though."

Percy's brow creased. "How so?"

"'Cause he was a surgeon, dude. He's had medical training. Plus, he is weird, right? That's not a figment of my imagination. Is it?"

"No, he's pretty weird."

"He's not married. Been single the entire time I've known him. Eats lunch by himself–that's a big one."

"Dude, you're not married and have been single for almost the entire time I've known you." He pointed to me, waving his finger in the air. "If that's your criteria, you're still on the suspect list."

"Dude. Seriously?"

"Dude." He chuckled. "All I'm saying is people can be single. That's not the only thing that makes him weird. I'm fucking single."

"You know what I mean. Don't be an idiot. And I'm dead serious about this. We should go to the police. Or call in an anonymous tip."

"We don't have any evidence. A guy having a couple certificates in his office doesn't mean shit. Even if he admitted killing someone; that was when he was a doctor. Doctors get away with killing people all the time. Anyway, look . . . you can't go off that stuff. You need proof. Something tangible. If you found an arm or a leg or something . . ."

I counted my *evidence* off on my fingers. "He's a recluse. He has a background in performing surgeries. He has this backstory about accidentally killing a person, which, by the way, is how every supervillain's backstory begins. They get a taste for murder by complete accident." I didn't actually believe this, but it sounded pretty good. "Maybe he has all this pent-up aggression and he takes it out on these women. He's not killing them. Just ruining them. He's–"

"Stop. You're reaching. You're reaching so far you've pulled a muscle."

"The evidence is there. If this were a character in one of your movies, wouldn't Glen be the obvious suspect?"

"Yeah, but the real killer is *never* the obvious suspect."

"But this isn't a fucking movie!"

Giving up, Percy threw his hands in the air. "Dude, if Glen ends up being the Hacketstown Hacker, I'll give you my next paycheck."

"For real?"

"Yeah."

"Deal."

We shook on it. He tossed me another beer.

"You should focus less on this Hacker thing, and more on Kayla. Have you told her the truth yet? Have you done anything to help the situation?"

I sipped the foamy rush building at the mouth of the can. "I'm working on it."

But I wasn't working on it.

I got home just before midnight and almost tripped over the unmarked package left on my stoop. Nearly fell to the concrete, and would have, had the railing not been within reach. I tucked the package under my arm and headed inside, shutting out the cold night.

I didn't think much of the package. It was a couple of weeks into the new year and I thought maybe it was a gift from a relative, an aunt or an uncle I haven't spoken to in some time. Which was kind of dumb looking back on it because I never got packages from family members, Christmas or any other celebratory holiday. Anyway, I plopped the thing down on the kitchen table and went about my night, making myself a late dinner, pouring myself another beer, and putting on Netflix, preparing for a late-night binge of whatever new series they'd come out with.

As I went to take my microwavable dinner out of the microwave, I noticed the package was leaking some dark substance onto the table. It dripped onto the floor, forming a small midnight-mauve puddle on the tile. I abandoned my meal and headed over to the mysterious package. I hadn't checked the sender's address.

If I had, I might have discovered the contents inside a lot sooner.

I ran my car key along the tape, opened the flaps, and let the smell out. *The smell*–it was awful, to say the least. Like roadkill and rotten fruit mixed together. My stomach turned and I immediately lost my appetite. The thought of eating now disgusted me, brought me to the verge of throwing up.

I didn't want to peek inside. I knew what the box most likely contained, given the smell and dark fluids, but I couldn't *not* look inside. I had to know. I had to put my eyes on it. I had to *see.*

It was a lot worse than I thought.

It was an arm, severed from the elbow down, the hand bent at the wrist on an impossible angle so the whole thing could fit inside. The dark fluid had been blood, obviously, mostly congealed by now, but still wet. It wasn't my first thought, but I did wonder how long ago the arm had been cut off. My first thought was: *holy shit, holy shit, holy fucking shit!* My second or third thought questioned *when* the act had taken place. Hours? Earlier in the day, that was for sure. The blood was still too fresh for it to have been any longer. The skin, though marred with blood and a savage, ragged wound where an elbow should have been, was only starting to lose its color, starting to gray.

I backed away, an instinctive move. Numbness came at my limbs with a surprising quickness, causing my knees to quiver uncontrollably. I thought I was headed for the floor. A part of me wished I had passed out, hit my head, and bled to death. How *the fuck* would I explain this to the police? It was a conversation that death seemed preferable to.

I reached for the phone in my pocket, my hands shaking like a dried-up alcoholic's. Before I dialed 911, I noticed a sticky note inside the box, tacked to the cardboard's interior. It contained a simple message: *A gift for you.*

My heart fell into my shoes. My nerves became a horde of insects buzzing around my body. My muscles felt like sacks of concrete, weighing me down. I dropped my phone on the tile, and didn't even care when a jagged crack split the screen in half. I put my hands on the table and leaned forward, doing everything I could to keep standing. The bottom had fallen out of the world and it felt like I was continuously falling, falling into an opaque void full of negative energy. A void with no end, no beginning, no middle. A place of no escape. A place that just simply . . . *was.*

Here I was, in that place.

The note rocked me.

A gift for you.

The implications shook me to the bone. This meant someone knew my secret. Someone knew my taste in women included sans an arm or two. And not just *any* someone–the motherfucking Hacketstown Hacker. This crushed me. I had been so careful. Been so secretive. I had told no one about my sex life, except recently. I had told three people; Percy, Wendy, and the least helpful shrink in town. I immediately dismissed the idea of the shrink being capable of such a thing, let alone being the Hacketstown Hacker. It wouldn't have made much sense at all. Same went for Wendy. Percy, on the other hand . . .

I guess he was a more likely candidate. Although, no–I couldn't see him as someone who'd cut the arm off an innocent person. Sure, he was into the whole horror scene, but that didn't automatically make him a full-blown psychopath. I briefly considered the possibility the arm was a fake, a movie prop, and Percy had sent me the "gift", but given the nature of our recent conversations, I didn't think that made much sense. Plus, there was the smell, and no one could ever replicate that pungent, ungodly odor.

No, this had come from someone else. A psychopath. A man (or a woman) who was going around the tri-county area and having himself a ball by snipping the limbs off innocent women.

A gift for you.

Those words ate away at my sanity.

A chill entered my system, freezing me from the inside out. The hair on my arms stood like blades of grass. I trembled from fear, afraid of what would come next.

I knew I had to phone the police. I *had to.*

But did I? What if I didn't? What if I took the arm and buried it in the small area outside the back of my apartment? What if I dumped it in the dumpster around the corner, behind Antonio's Pizza? The possible places I could ditch the severed arm were almost endless.

But what if I were caught? There would be no talking my way

out of it. No reasonable excuse would satisfy a curious mind.

Something about sweeping this under the rug felt wrong. I'd become very good at hiding secrets over the years, but this wasn't one I wanted to bury.

I called 911.

And waited for help to arrive.

Two detectives arrived twenty minutes later. Twenty minutes after that, my apartment was flooded by the local police force. The entire complex was lit with flashing red and blue lights. I doubted there was anyone left at the station. They began roping the area off with yellow caution tape, and then assaulted me with a litany of questions. *When did you discover the package? Do you know anyone who might have done this? Seen anything strange around your apartment complex? Do you have any enemies, Mr. Bridges? What time did you get home again?*

My neighbors received the same treatment, somewhat to a greater degree since they were home all day and might have seen who had dropped off the package. But, of course, no one had seen anything or anyone. No one at all. They were pretty useless, but the police thanked them for their contributions anyway, and they were told to call the number on the card if they happened to remember anything, anything at all, down to the smallest detail. They were assured the most minor tidbit could lead to a big break.

The police led me back inside, told me to pack an overnight bag, maybe two or three days' worth of clothes. I thought this was a bit unnecessary, seeing as the crime took place on my porch and not inside my apartment, but they were the fucking police and who was I to argue.

I didn't exactly feel like spending money on a goddamn hotel room, though. The only place near me was an overpriced chain, and the only other option was the little love shacks down by the lakes, a cluster of one-room cabins that were dirtier than the earth they'd been built upon. No way I was paying to stay there. In fact, I didn't think I'd stay there if *they* were paying *me*.

I made a phone call to Percy. He didn't pick up. Not shocking. He was probably in the middle of a beer coma. I thought about heading over to his house anyway, knocking on his door, even if it would wake up his folks. This was an emergency and I was sure they'd understand. But before I did that, I tapped another number on my now-cracked phone screen.

Kayla's.

It was a long shot. A real Hail Mary, but I had to chance it.

Unexpectedly, she picked up on the second ring.

"Well, this is a surprise," she answered, sounding none too happy about it.

"Hopefully a pleasant one," I said, sounding full of hope and promise.

"Not exactly."

"Ouch."

"What do you want?"

"Well, the craziest thing just happened."

"Hm. I bet."

"Yeah, so someone mailed a severed limb to my apartment and now it's a crime scene and the police are digging through it and kicking me out. You know. An average Tuesday night."

"Are you serious? Because if you're not serious, that's the worst booty call line I've ever heard. And I've heard them all."

I ignored the *booty call* stuff. "You think I'd joke about that?"

"Yeah, I do."

"You're right. I probably would. But I'm not." I tore the phone away from my ear, opened the camera app, and snapped a picture, sending her a shot of the commotion taking place at the apartment complex, the swarm of men and women in blue uniforms. "See? The police are having a party at my place and I'm not invited."

She paused, checking the pic. "Holy shit."

"Yeah, that's what I said when I came home to a severed arm on my porch."

"Who the hell sent you a severed arm?"

"Wish I knew, but I suspect it's what the police are here to find out."

She got quiet. "Why are you calling *me* of all people?"

"Because. . ." I scratched the back of my neck. Asking her would be awkward no matter how I went about it, so I didn't think about it and spoke the first words that came to mind. ". . . I was hoping your parents had a couch I could occupy for the night."

"Really?"

"I know, I'm sorry. But Percy isn't picking up his phone and I don't want to stay in the love shacks–"

"The love shacks?"

"Yeah, it's a small cluster of cabins down near the lakes. They are usually rented at an hourly rate. Which is why people call them the love shacks."

"Interesting . . ."

"I've never been myself, but I hear they're lovely this time of year. And by *lovely* I mean covered in semen."

"Gross. But I guess it could be worse."

"What's worse than sleeping on a bed coated with random strangers' dried semen?"

"I dunno. Sleeping out in the cold. In the woods somewhere. Dying of hypothermia?"

"I guess . . . but not worse by much. Maybe a smidge."

"It's weird you use words like 'smidge.'"

"That's me. Pretty weird." I paused, waiting for her to invite me over. "Sooooo . . . about that couch."

"You know, cars can be pretty comfortable. The seats recline. I think you can make do with that. As far as I know, your seats aren't coated with semen. Are they?"

"Not currently."

"So gross."

"You asked."

Another pause. Another hopeful moment where I waited for her to meet me halfway. I was trying to initiate the spark again, and I thought I was doing a pretty damn good job.

Finally: "You can't sleep on the couch."

"Damn."

"My parents are asleep and they'll freak out if some strange man is on their couch when they wake up in the morning."

"Okay . . ."

"So," she said, sighing simultaneously, "it'll have to be my bed."

"Really?"

"Yes. I'll leave the bedroom window open. Hope you're good at climbing trees."

She hung up.

I hadn't climbed a tree since grade school, but I was pretty sure I'd be great at it. Motivation is a hell of a drug.

TWENTY-ONE

THE climb up to Kayla's window went a lot easier than I expected. I had to shimmy my way up the trunk, but once I was able to grab the branches, the rest of the way was a breeze. Transitioning from the branches to the window had been challenging, but Kayla saw me, rushed over, and lifted the window sash to help me inside.

I tumbled across her floor with the grace of a walrus.

She shushed me.

"Sorry," I said, brushing the loose bark off the inside of my pant legs.

"My parents are light sleepers," she whispered.

"That doesn't bode well for us then, does it?"

"We'll just have to be quiet."

I followed her lead, whispering too. "I guess no talking then?"

"Whispering only." She smiled. It wasn't a smile I'd expected to see. Then again, I didn't expect her to invite me in like a vampire on the prowl for familiar blood. I didn't deserve to be here. I had broken it off with her with almost no explanation, ripped her heart out and stomped on it, and she was still kind enough to take me in.

"You're twenty-five. Do your parents honestly care if you have boys over?"

She nodded slowly. "My dad would kill me. Well, maybe you. Not me. I'm his little princess."

"Suddenly a semen-crusted mattress sounds a lot better."

She stifled a giggle. "Come here."

She took the sides of my head with her hands, brought me closer to her. The space between us narrowed at a snail's pace, but I didn't mind–I was staring into her eyes, getting lost within them, the tunnels leading to her intentions. Her pupils twinkled in the reflection of the moon.

Our lips touched. Pressed together, we hardly kissed, at least at first. We sort of just let our skin meet. Then she opened her mouth and I felt the warmth of her breath, the wet of her tongue. I returned with some tongue of my own.

There we stood, in the center of her room (immaculately kept by the way), devouring each other's mouths. The January weather crept in from the open window, sending a harsh chill down my back. I didn't want to, but I pulled away.

"Let me close the window," I said, and started toward the rush of arctic wind.

She didn't let me break our connection. Yanking me back to her, she smashed her face into mine. The collision didn't hurt as much as it surprised me. She opened her mouth and clamped onto mine, not losing a single step. Then she pushed me on her bed. Took off her shirt. Helped me with mine.

"Do you have a condom?" she asked.

I didn't even think to bring one. "No," I said, embarrassed.

Her head drooped, her long hair falling over her disappointed reaction.

"Are you clean?" she asked.

"Am I clean?"

"Yes." A coy glance. "You know what I mean."

"Oh, yeah. I get checked all the time." Not far from the truth, but I'd been tested a few months back. "I'm clean."

"Okay," she said. "Then fuck it."

She dropped to her knees and began to unbuckle my pants. The room was still cold, but not as cold as it had been standing in front of the window. Within seconds, my pants and boxers were around my ankles. She took me into her mouth. It felt good. Real good. I closed my eyes. Imagined her doing the same thing, only without an arm. Or both legs. As she worked up and down my cock with her tongue, I moaned softly. Not enough to wake her parents, so I hoped.

She kept sucking and I kept my eyes pinched shut, trying to imagine what she'd look like with no arms, bouncing up and down on me, my hard dick slipping in and out of her wet vagina.

(a severed arm in the box, pink tufts of muscle poking out of the ragged, torn flesh)

My eyes flipped opened and I must have seemed shocked.

She took my penis out of her mouth and rested it on her cheek. "What's the matter?" she asked, smiling devilishly.

"Nothing," I said, breathing heavily. "Keep going."

She did.

I closed my eyes.

This time, I saw Glen standing over her corpse.

(Myriad limbs hanging from the ceiling like bags of meat in a slaughterhouse freezer. Glen, arching his back, laughing into the cool air above him. Glen letting the chainsaw rip, buzz with authority. Glen lowering the angry teeth into Kayla's soft, dead flesh. Blood sputtering like mud from under a stuck tire.)

I went soft in her mouth.

Her eyes filled with concern. She kept working, but to no avail. She brought both hands into the equation, which just made things worse.

"Is . . ." she said, her playful smile eroding. "Is everything all right?"

I shook my head, knowing full well this wasn't going to work. "I'm sorry."

She stopped tugging on my flaccid penis and stood up, walked over to where she'd shed her clothes, and began dressing.

"God, Kayla, I'm so fucking sorry."

She put her finger over her lips, then continued slipping her pajamas back on. After she was comfortable, she strolled over to the bed, sat behind me, and wrapped her arms around my naked chest. She kissed my ear. Squeezed me like a child would her teddy bear.

"It's okay," she whispered into my ear. "Come."

I turned to her. She pecked my lips. A shiver ran down my spine, but it had nothing to do with the open window. I lay down next to her and she held my hands.

"I love you," she whispered, taking my hands and pressing them against her chest. I felt the thrum of her heartbeat on my knuckles. "Whatever's wrong, we can fix it."

I almost fucking cried.

She kissed me again. Before sleep came for us, we stared into each other's eyes for a long time.

When I closed my eyes, it was dark. When I opened them, light flooded my vision. So much light. The sun beamed through the open window. I sat up, vaguely aware of my location. It took about three seconds to realize I wasn't in my apartment. The events of last night slowly came back to me, and, sitting there, I saw them clearly. A flare of embarrassment flashed under my cheeks, burning the back of my neck.

Shit, I can't believe that happened. I cursed myself for being so fucking weird, such a freak. All I wanted was to be normal. To be able to enjoy a nice, romantic evening with Kayla. None of this would be happening to me if I were normal. None of it.

I looked to the empty space on the bed where Kayla had been when I closed my eyes. Then I felt something sticky on my forehead. Reaching for it, a pang of uneasiness swept through me. I imagined Kayla's father busting into her room, a hatchet in hand, ready to take off my head. Then, I thought more sensibly—Kayla was probably downstairs explaining the situation to them. Maybe they weren't as bad as she'd made them out to be. Maybe she'd told me to sneak in through her window because she wanted to sleep with me. A clever tactic, nothing more.

The longer I thought about it, the more sense that made.

The thing on my forehead was a yellow sticky note. It read: WENT TO WORK. USE THE WINDOW. - K.

There was a little smiley face at the bottom, which was good. Promising. Let me know she wasn't mad, that last night left the door open. Kept me hopeful we still had something, the flame hadn't blown out, especially after last night's lackluster performance. Maybe, just maybe, we had a future.

(Kayla in pieces, her parts littered across the floor of one of those love shacks near the lake. Glen standing over her, raising a katana above his head, screaming victoriously, like he'd conquered enemy territory, like he'd washed the lands in their blood.)

Glen. I needed to get to him. Find him. Make him admit he was the Hacketstown Hacker.

What I'd do after that was still up for debate.

Glen, would you mind making Kayla your next victim? Pretty please? I'll never give you another attitude at work ever again. EV-ER. I'll even stop stacking the Blu-rays on their side like I know you hate but do it anyway because I KNOW you hate it. Pretty please with severed fingers on top?

No, I couldn't do that. Could I? Could I do that to Kayla, especially after she'd taken last night so . . . so well? Could I ruin her life just so we could continue our romantic entanglement? What if it didn't work with us? What if we broke up later on down the road? Then she'd be sans a limb all because of me and my stupid condition. She'd have to live out the rest of her life without an arm or a leg and maybe—just maybe—no one would love her, not the way I would. Who was I kidding? Someone would love her. She was perfect. Limbs or no limbs, she was fucking perfect.

I couldn't do that to her.

Could I?

I am not a monster.

Whatever I would decide, the first thing was to get out of her house quietly so her parents wouldn't hear me. I heard a bump down the hall, two voices, and then decided that was my cue to get out, and fast.

TWENTY-TWO

"YOU what now?"

"Percy, do you even listen to me when I talk?" I'd been driving home when Percy called. I'd told him everything about last night, everything from the present on my porch to my failed attempt to have sex with Kayla.

"I'm sorry, I just can't tell if you're joking or not."

"Does it sound like I'm joking?"

He waited a few seconds before answering, as if he actually thought I'd make light of what happened. "No, I don't. But, dude. What the fuck?"

"Whoever this person is, knows about me. Knows my secrets."

"A gift for you."

"Exactly." Just thinking about it, seeing those words burned into my mind, made my skin prickle with fear. "I only told three people in my entire life. The shrink, this chick Wendy, and *you.*"

"Dude . . ." His voice cracked. For a second, I thought that was all he had to say on the topic. "You don't actually think I—"

"No, I don't."

"Good. Because I'm not. That'd be fucked up."

"Yes, it would."

"So who do you think it is? Still Glen?"

"It's the only logical assumption. He has the medical training history, we can both agree he's a pretty big weirdo, and . . . he knows me."

"But he doesn't know you like to fuck amputees."

"Can you not put it like that?"

"How should I put it?"

"I dunno . . . not . . . not like that."

"Okay, fine. Then he doesn't know you like to make love to people with certain disabilities."

"Better, but not by much."

"Okay, dude. Listen, I can't censor your weird fetish. I'm just going to call it as I see it."

"Firstly, it's not weird. I find these women attractive and beautiful, and there's nothing weird about that, it's . . . goddammit, I thought I explained all of this to you already."

"You did, and I'm still adjusting. Bear with me."

"Fine."

"So, whatever. Bottom line: Glen the Best Tronics Master Dickhead does *not* know about your *thing*."

I cringed. "Don't call it a *thing* now."

"I'm literally two seconds away from hanging up on you."

"Okay, okay. Just . . . I see your point."

"Okay. Yeah, so . . . where does that leave us?"

"He could have overheard us talking about it or something."

"In my garage over beers? I think we would have noticed if our manager was sneaking around my stepdad's place in the middle of the day."

"Maybe. Did we mention it at work?"

"I don't think so."

I wasn't sure if we had or not. Maybe he'd caught me throwing up behind the store. Did Percy mention my acrotomophilia then? Fuck. I couldn't remember. No, that was before I told him. Had to be. I had fed him a line about having too much sushi. Then how did he figure it out? How the fuck did he know?

My head was beginning to spin. The road markings began to twist and arch, the solid yellow line bending like a frequency wavelength. Suddenly, I felt like I needed to pull over, throw up.

"You still there, dude?" Percy asked, and I could sense the

concern in his voice.

"Yeah, still here." I coasted onto the shoulder, ignoring the beeping from behind. I must've been driving erratically, swerving between lanes, but I didn't care. I was trying to avoid having a goddamn heart attack. "We have to call the cops."

"On Glen?"

"Yes, on Glen. Haven't you been following the conversation?"

"Man, I dunno. It just doesn't feel right."

I stopped on the side of the road and pinched the bridge of my nose, unable to process how Percy wasn't connecting all the dots. "He's our guy. He's our Hacketstown Hacker."

"Still willing to bet he's not, but whatever."

"All right, I'm on my way in. Is Glen there?"

"No, but he should be in a little bit."

"Okay. Have you seen Kayla?"

"Mmmmm . . . I don't think so. She working today?"

"Yes, she left for work about an hour ago."

"Nope, can't say I've seen her."

An intense pang of panic boomed in my chest. It wasn't like Percy worked in the stockroom; he worked the floor and he should have seen her by now.

"Are you sure?"

"Yeah, man. Pretty sure."

"Shit."

"What is it?"

"Dude, she should have been there by now."

"Well, maybe she's here and I didn't see her."

"Purse."

"What?"

I turned the key, cranked the engine. Pulling back onto the highway, I lowered the gas pedal to the floor.

"Go see if she clocked in and text me. I'm on my way."

My heart punched the walls of my chest so hard I thought it would surely break. Explode. Cause me to drive into the guardrail. Kill me.

Pulling into the parking lot, I controlled my breathing. In through my nose, out through my mouth. Slow. Regulated. Carefully managed. My heart rate slowed, but not by much.

I practically ran into work.

As soon as I made it through the sliding glass doors, Percy was there to greet me.

"She's not here, man," he said, sounding alarmed, which triggered more irregular movements in my chest.

"Fuck!" I practically shouted. A few people looked my way, but I wasn't in my Best Tronics uniform, so I hardly cared. I wouldn't have cared either way; my nerves were on fire and I didn't feel in control of my bodily functions, especially my mouth. "We have to call the police," I said, glancing around. "Tell them everything we know about Glen and the Hacketstown Hacker."

"Pump the brakes, kid. First off, we don't even know she's . . . whatever you think she is."

"Missing? Abducted? It's pretty fucking obvious she's been taken. Her car isn't at home and it's not here. On the way in, something must have happened." I dialed her number, put it on speaker, and listened to it go directly to voicemail. "See? Now her phone is off. Before it was ringing."

"Maybe she turned it off."

"Why would she turn it off?"

"I dunno. Maybe the battery died."

"It's eleven o'clock."

"Maybe it didn't charge last night? Maybe she was too busy taking care of your sorry ass? Or maybe the wire popped out, didn't get a full charge. Now it's dead. Shit happens to me all the time."

I shook my head. I couldn't understand why Percy was playing devil's advocate, but it made me want to punch him. "Why are you fighting me on this?"

"I'm not fighting you . . . I just think we shouldn't jump to any rash decisions. I mean, you have to admit, you've been acting a little off since this whole Kayla thing began. First you tell me about the acroto-toe-en thingy—"

"Acrotomophilia," I corrected.

"Yeah, that. Next, you think Glen is the Hacketstown Hacker. Now, Kayla is magically missing. I dunno, man. That's a lot going on."

I leered at him. "What are you saying? I'm making this all up?"

"No, no, no." He pumped his hands, begging me to kill the thought. "No, not at all. I think you've just been a little stressed out lately, wound up. Maybe this acro-toe-mo-philia thing has something to do with it. Like, maybe you're discovering that's a part of you you no longer want, and now you're dealing with it face-to-face and maybe, just maybe, it's affecting you in a certain way. Mentally, that is. Scrambling you all up."

I stared at him, not sure if I should reason with him or just knock him upside his head. "Percy. Listen to me. Please, God, listen to me. This is not the result of anything other than me piecing together the facts that have been presented before us." Leaning into his ear, I whispered, "Kayla *is* missing. Glen took her because he *is* the Hacketstown Hacker."

He stood there frozen, his gaze lifting. Over me. Past me.

"Is there a problem, Bridges?" asked a voice, one familiar. One that chilled my core.

I turned and saw Glen standing there, pushing his glasses up his nose. In his other hand, he held his brown-bagged lunch. He didn't seem too happy with what he'd discovered walking into work.

Me. Talking about him. Claiming him to be the Hacketstown Hacker.

"Nope," I said. "Nothing."

"Good." He checked his watch. "Better clock in, Bridges. Wouldn't want you to be late."

TWENTY-THREE

IT was the slowest work day ever. I must have taken about fifty mini-breaks so I could hide out in the stockroom and try Kayla's phone. No answer. Nothing. Still went right to voicemail. I asked Martin, the other assistant manager, if he'd taken a call out from her, and he had told me no, he hadn't. He also told me he phoned her parents, who also weren't answering at home. I was at a complete loss. No one, none of the other cashiers, knew anything about her no-call, no-show.

In the parking lot, standing rigidly in the forty-degree sunshine, sweat poured off me. I began to pace, slowly at first, but as my anxiety cranked up to about eleven, I was really moving. Back and forth. Continuing to call her cell, even though I knew she wouldn't pick up. Just hearing her recorded voice injected my nerves with further panic.

Percy put his arm out in front of him like a stop sign. "Dude, you're going to kill yourself at this rate."

"I can't sit around and wait anymore. We have to do something."

Surrendering, Percy tossed his hands in the air. "Okay, man. I'll humor you. What do you want me to do?"

"Let's call the cops."

"We did that already."

Sort of. Earlier today, a detective called me, telling me it was okay to use my apartment again, they'd collected all the evidence they needed. They didn't give me any details beyond that, even when I asked. I brought up Kayla, her sudden disappearance, and the douchebag detective didn't seem too concerned about it. He asked if she was a minor. I said *no.* Asked if we had had a fight. I said *no.* Then he asked if we were living together, to which I also replied *no.* He told me if she wasn't a minor, there was nothing I could do for at least forty-eight hours.

Two days. Two *goddamn* days.

I had told him that was unacceptable, but again, he brushed off my concerns, saying, "I don't know what to tell you, kid. That's how we handle things. I hope your girlfriend turns up. If she doesn't, call me back and I'll help you fill out the report myself."

That had been his only advice; and he hung up.

"We should call the police on Glen. Get them to show up at his house. Get them to investigate. Search the premises. Surely they'll find evidence of something. Especially if Kayla's there."

"And how the hell do you suppose we do that?"

"Call in an anonymous tip. Tell them we saw Glen dragging a body into his house."

"That's original."

"You got something better?"

"Hm. A cold IPA and *Hell Night* on Blu-ray?"

I bit my tongue till it hurt.

Percy dropped his arms, letting them hang at his side. "Fine. I'll go through with your little idea. But only if you take the blame when we get caught for phoning in a phony report."

Tapping my chest, I said, "I'll take full responsibility."

"Good. So, then, what's the plan?"

We'd dialed 911 from the only known payphone in the entire town—out in front of a 7-Eleven on the west end of town. I'd told them we were one of Glen's neighbors, we'd seen him come home late that evening and it looked like he'd taken a girl out of his trunk, brought her inside. I said the girl looked dead, but I couldn't be sure from my vantage point. The operator tried to keep me on the line, but I'd made up an excuse ("I have to take out the trash") and hung up.

After, we'd left the scene and drove off, killing our headlights in case there were cameras in the parking lot. Then we hit the highway, heading over to the address I had given the operator, the one I'd lifted from the store's database.

Now, we crouched in a small wooded area across from Glen's home, dressed in all black. We let the shadows protect us from late-night dog-walkers, joggers, and passing cars. The streetlights left illuminated puddles on the street, making the shadows (and us) appear even darker. There were a few lights on in Glen's house, and we'd seen him zip by the bay window several times during our stakeout, which was turning into a longer ordeal than I predicted. It had been almost an hour since I'd called in the suspicious activity, and there were still no signs of the police.

"Think they came already?" Percy asked in a hushed voice.

"No, no way. It only took us ten minutes to get here. No way the cops are that fast. Not in this town anyway."

It was true. In the past, we'd gotten a few drunks who'd come into the store after getting kicked out of a nearby bar. Only a few times this happened, but every time we called the police, they'd taken their sweet-ass time getting there. By the time they had shown up, the drunkards were stumbling down the street or well on their way home via their friendly neighborhood Uber driver.

Couldn't count on the police for anything, at least here. I'd hate to think if there were an actual emergency.

And to me, this *was* an actual emergency.

"Look," Percy said, tapping my shoulder.

Down the street, headlights turned the corner.

I breathed a sigh of relief. "About fucking time."

The cruiser parked against the curb. Two officers got out, both of them looking a lot younger than the two of us.

Great, I thought, *they sent a pair of rookies.* I didn't want to judge a book by its cover, but come on. These guys had no idea what they were walking into.

What are they walking into? I asked myself.

I pictured a basement full of scattered human body parts, appendages of all shapes and sizes, most of them deteriorated from advanced stages of decay. I imagined them being used for art, preserved, the centerpiece of a colorful arrangement of flowers or artsy design. Craft projects where the human flesh and bone and dead tissue were used to create something beautiful, unique, and tragic. Something that told a grotesque story using only demented visuals. Dioramas where hands and feet were stationed in the middle of the rainforest or prehistoric times, the subjects crafted to look like trees, animals, one of Earth's natural imperfections.

I pushed these morbid thoughts aside and concentrated on the scene unfolding before me. Even though my focus was precisely on Kayla and finding her safe, I could still smell the potential malodor coming from Glen's basement; it reeked like death, the rotting of lost limbs.

Glen had answered the door, smiling but worried. Any time a cop shows up at your doorstep, it's never to present you with the winning lottery ticket. I mean, it did happen once in a Nicolas Cage movie, but that was . . . well, a movie.

Glen nodded, listening to the cops. One of them explained the situation, pointing to different areas of the property while the other one migrated down the porch, helping himself to a look around. Glen played it cool, not paying attention to the other officer, opting to listen to the explanation of why they were here. After a few minutes of them going back and forth, trading words (which we couldn't hear), Glen stepped aside and invited them in.

We watched the two cops enter and Glen shut the door behind them.

"Holy shit," Percy said. "It worked."

I didn't share his enthusiasm. Letting them in without protest meant he had nothing to hide, and him having nothing to hide meant . . . well, it likely meant he had nothing to hide.

"Fuck," I whispered.

"What? This is good. A lot further than I would have guessed. Honestly, I thought the cops weren't even going to show up."

"I don't like it."

Three minutes later, the cops emerged from the house. They walked down the steps without a hitch in their gait, both of them heading toward their cruiser. From the open doorway, Glen called out something that sounded a lot like, "Have a good night!" and waved.

One of the officers, the passenger, threw up a hand in reply, but the other kept walking, listening to the dispatcher who was informing him of a "ten-thirty-five" somewhere in the area.

Glen stood on his porch and saw them off. Once they were clear, he gritted his teeth and shook his head, stormed back inside and slammed the door behind him. I swear I heard him say something about "fucking cocksuckers", but I couldn't be one-hundred-percent sure. In any case, he was pissed. Beyond pissed. I was actually surprised the door didn't crack because the impact carried down the street, sounding off like a clap of thunder.

Percy and I looked at each other, each of us holding the same confused expression.

"Well," Percy said, gulping, "I'm guessing you have a backup plan."

"Actually," I said, cracking my knuckles. "I do."

TWENTY-FOUR

"NO way," he said, stomping his feet on the blacktop. "No. Fucking. Way."

"Come on," I pleaded, "you said you were gonna see this through."

"That didn't include breaking into my assistant manager's house while he's fucking sleeping." His arm shot out and he extended his forefinger at Glen's quiet, suburban ranch. "*If* he fucking sleeps. Who knows what time his head'll hit the pillow."

"He opens tomorrow. He'll be in bed soon."

"So you hope."

"Dude, trust me."

"I don't trust you. Your behavior is making you erratic as fuck lately. Seriously, man. The entire time I've known you, you've never behaved like this. You were always the calm one. Cool and collected. Hell, you hardly spoke a word your first three weeks at Best Tronics. High school? Man, you were always the kid in the back of the class who never made a peep unless the teacher called on you." His head shook like a chill had crawled up his vertebrae. "What the hell happened to you?"

Staring into the black, starry night behind him, I thought about it. Or at least pretended to think about it, pretended I was conjuring up some good response to satisfy him, something reasonable, considering my recent actions. But I already knew the answer and I was deliberately stalling, trying to think of the best way to describe everything I'd been feeling over the last few weeks. In the end, I only needed one word: "Love."

Percy's eyes widened with not-quite rage, but something else. It was an innocent gesture, a natural response. It was the genuine reaction to someone who's never been there. "Love?"

"Yeah, love."

"What do you mean . . . *love.*"

"I mean what I said. Love. Do I have to elaborate?"

"I mean . . . love is just . . . not much of an answer."

I grabbed my friend by the shoulders and actually almost laughed when he flinched. "Percy. You're my best friend, and quite honestly, my *only* friend. Only good one, I guess. Now, I know you've never met someone, I know you've never experienced what I have over the last three weeks . . . but one day you will and you will understand, and when you do . . . goddamn, it'll be a magical moment in your life."

A goofy smile spread across his face, and his eyes darted elsewhere. "Okay . . ."

I hugged him. "You're a great friend, man."

"Okay . . ." he said, not hugging me back. "Still not going in there with you."

I let go. "I understand."

"You're going? In there? Alone?"

"Yes."

"There's nothing in there. The cops were—"

I shushed him. "I have to. Even if she's not in there, I have to go with my gut. This feels right to me. This feels . . . I dunno. I can sense her. She's close."

"What? Dude, first off, you don't have superpowers. You can't possibly know—"

"Sssh. Trust me."

He shook his head. "I'm heading back to the car." He'd parked two streets over and we had walked. He began his trek back to his Camry. "You coming or not?"

"No."

"You're really going in there?"

I stared at him blankly.

"How you getting home?"

"I'll Uber."

He raised his hand in the air. "Well, it was nice working with you. Don't call me for bail money."

"Percy," I said.

He stopped backpedaling.

"Thank you for coming this far."

"Don't do anything stupid. Please?"

I winked at him.

Things were about to get really fucking stupid.

I waited another hour in the bushes. The lights had gone off inside the house before Percy left, so I was fairly certain Glen had gone to bed. Only the porch lights remained on, and I was pretty sure they weren't going off any time soon. Glen struck me as a leave-my-lights-on-all-night kinda guy.

I hustled across the street and shot down the alley between the house and a long row of neatly hedged bushes. Making my way into the backyard, I crouched down and waited for my eyes to adjust to the darkness. There were no lights back there, and thankfully none were powered by motion-sensing technology, which surprised me considering he managed a Best Tronics and was able to secure a pretty hefty discount at his employment level. I thought his house would be decked out in the newest home security equipment, but I was proven wrong.

I hoped I wouldn't be proven wrong about my other speculations.

I hoped Kayla was somewhere inside. Actually, I didn't hope that. I hoped she was at home, prayed she was in bed, not suffering from any of the things that traveled my thoughts, the horrible images I found there. I wished she hadn't gotten caught up in this madness. This insanity was slowly becoming my fault. The Hackettstown Hacker knew who I was, knew my secret, and he'd gone after Kayla for . . . what exactly?

My gift for you . . .

Oh Jesus. The thought of Glen hacking off her arm at the

shoulder made me want to puke all over his flowerbed.

I had to stop this.

But what if you don't?

I couldn't possibly sit idle.

What if you let it happen?

I couldn't do that to her.

But it's what you want, isn't it?

I didn't want her life ruined for the sake of my penis, my deeply psychological sex issues.

It will solve all your problems.

I love her. I can't . . . allow this . . .

You'll be happy.

She'll be miserable.

The voice stopped. I'd beaten it, convinced it to go away. I continued kneeling in darkness, waiting for my thoughts to conclude their song, and within twenty seconds, they did. I faced the backyard. Reduced to shadowy moonlight, I was able to make my way down the alley and turn the corner, nearly tripping over the basement's metal Bilco doors.

I reached for the handle, grabbed the padlock instead.

Dammit.

I didn't expect Glen to leave his house unlocked, open for anyone to just come waltzing through. The back door was surely the same, *locked,* and it looked like the only way inside would be breaking the glass, reaching inside and unlocking the deadbolt. It was that, or find some way to knock off the padlock on the Bilco door. I didn't think I could do either without waking up a neighbor. Or Glen.

But I needed a way in. Kayla was inside. I knew it. I could feel her energy, feel her pulse through the walls. It was like our bodies were connected, as if we shared a single existence. Our heartbeats throbbed as one. I closed my eyes and found myself staring into hers. In my mental image, she was smiling—always smiling—and happy to see my face. Her hands reached for my cheeks and she rested her palms there, a gentle touch that funneled a heavenly sensation into my heart. She brought her lips to mine. Kissed. Eyes closed. We tasted each other.

Opening my eyes, I found myself back in the dark. My hand

searched the nearby flowerbed for something, anything I could use to break glass or the lock. I uncovered a rock about the size of a softball, perfect for smashing things, especially something as thin as the nine-lite glass in the door. My only concern was the sound it would make. And Christ, what if he had an alarm system? The second I'd smash in the glass, the police would be on their way.

I took a step back, rethinking my strategy. First, I planned my escape in case an alarm *did* sound. The wooden fence to my right was easily jumpable, and so were the fences beyond it. I could hop my way back to the main road like a bunny through a garden. Phone an Uber or hide in some bushes once I got there.

Busting the glass was almost a sure way to get myself caught. The lock, which looked tougher to break than the window, seemed like the quieter option. Also, I was almost certain he hadn't alarmed the basement doors. Could have been wrong, but I was willing to take a chance.

I went to work on the lock, striking down on it with the heavy rock in hand. The noise was louder than I had expected. The impact caused small sparks between the two objects. The rock and lock clanged on impact, a hollow, tinny thud. Not loud, but loud enough I suspected, if sensitive ears were afoot.

I ignored the noise. I concentrated on Kayla's face. Her smile. The warmth provided by her gaze, a three-second long joining of our eyes. I imagined her there with me, by my side, pulling this off with her support. I could almost feel her hand on my back, rubbing, calming me, keeping a full-fledged panic attack at bay.

Sweat dripped off me in rivers. Despite the chilly weather, the pocket between my first layer of clothing and my flesh was a sauna. I hit the lock in the sweet spot at just the right angle and it jingled loose. Quickly, I unhooked it from the hole and tossed it aside.

Opened the doors. Headed down into a deeper darkness, where no light seemed to shine.

I felt a lot like Dante crossing over into the Ninth Circle of Hell.

The only light in the basement came from the glow of my phone. Before making my way to the stairs on the opposite end, I took a quick survey, making sure Kayla and the other missing girls weren't tied up down here, or kept in cages, or chained to the walls, or whatever sick method Glen used to contain his hostages before slicing them up like Christmas hams.

But there was nothing down there. A bunch of boxes, over-stuffed with junk, stuff that could've easily been tossed out or sold at a yard sale. They towered pretty high, almost as tall as me. A few bookshelves. Some art, canvas paintings and photographs of well-known landscapes, clung to the concrete walls, which were painted some neutral color. Couldn't exactly tell because everything had an electric blue tinge to it, my phone tainting everything its light touched. There was a small workout station in the corner, a couple of free weights and a lift bench.

But no women.

No girls.

No parts dangling from the ceiling. No rusted tools speckled with familiar blood.

Nothing but your usual household items, nothing but ordinary stuff.

I made my way to the stairs and started up them. Stopped when I put my weight on the first step, listening to how loud the damned thing creaked. It was loud enough to wake up anyone in the house, even if someone was asleep on the second floor. Louder than me smashing the rock against the padlock, for sure.

I froze, listened for movement upstairs.

There wasn't any.

I tried another step. Equally loud.

But again, no one stirred. At least, I didn't hear anything.

Then I moved up the stairs, taking one at a time, slowly, careful not to put my full weight on any one step. When I reached the top, I pressed my ear to the door. There was light seeping in from underneath, hardly bright, but present. Maybe a nightlight or a dimmer cranked all the way down. I listened for something, *someone*, a voice or a footfall. But again . . . there was only silence in the house of Glen.

The door opened, gave way to the kitchen. I peeked inside, my eyes taking in the view of each open doorway, each shadowy corner where the Hacketstown Hacker could be hiding. Alert that I could be stepping into a trap, I moved away from the basement stairs and into the kitchen. I rotated as I walked, not spending more than three seconds facing one particular direction. When I felt I was "in the clear", I stopped and listened some more.

Nothing.

I calmed down a bit after that, realizing I'd successfully broken in without disturbing Glen's sleep. So I glanced around the kitchen, seeing if there were any signs of murder, Hacketstown Hacker evidence. And . . .

. . . and there wasn't.

Actually, he'd kept the place pretty immaculate. The sink was empty, the granite countertops free from even a speck of leftover food. Not a single crumb or dried droplet. I opened cabinets and drawers and found nothing out of place, no knives or other dining utensils speckled with dark brown blood. I rummaged through his pantry and saw nothing but the usual household snacks, a small stack of bottled water. His fridge was relatively clean, the worst offense being a quart of leftover chicken lo mein beginning to cultivate a funky odor. No severed limbs in there, no arms or legs packaged in plastic wrap.

I shut the fridge and turned around.

An explosion of light blinded me. Throwing my arm over my eyes, I backed into the fridge and slid to the floor.

I was fucking toast.

"What the fuck!" I heard myself cry out. Fear had spoken for me; the fear of being caught.

"Bridges?" an angry voice asked.

Cracking my eyelids, I squinted against the bright light. I could make out just enough of Glen's face to know he was seething, beyond pissed. I saw the whites of his teeth, his cheeks quivering with red anger.

"Bridges," he said again, confirming his suspicion.

My vision opened a little more, adjusting. The lights dimmed. More of Glen's body made its way into view.

Then I heard a click.

Glen stepped forward.

The barrel of a shotgun greeted me.

"Bridges," Glen said one more time, before taking aim at my head.

TWENTY-FIVE

"WHAT the fuck are you doing inside my house?" Glen asked, the shotgun trembling in his hands. "Did you . . . did you break in here?" He sounded confused. "Did I leave a door unlocked?" Panicked, now.

I kept my mouth shut.

"Answer me!" he shouted, and the gun bucked in his hands.

For a second, I thought I was gone, that my head had been reduced to a pulpy smear on the face of the refrigerator. But I didn't hear the weapon's thunderous boom. A few seconds passed and I was still alive. Sweating. But alive. My heart beating its way toward a heart attack. But alive.

"Bridges, what the hell are you doing in my house?" His expression changed, like something came to him—an epiphany. "Wait. You called the cops on me, didn't you? You told them I . . . you told them you saw me carry something inside that looked like a body?"

I swallowed what felt like a boulder. My mouth was dry and cottony. "Yes . . . yes, I did."

"Why?" His face twisted with a bit of confusion, his mouth hanging open, bottom lip curled inward. "Why would you do this to me? Is it . . . is it because of your review? I mean, it was hardly a bad one. I've given worse. In fact, I thought it was quite positive."

He was playing dumb. A rush of anger spiked my nerves. "Where is she?"

His eyes darted across the room, back and forth. Up and down. The ceiling. The floor. "What in God's name are you talking about?"

"Kayla. I want to know where you're keeping her. The other girls, too."

He lowered the shotgun. "Kayla? You think she's here?"

"Don't play dumb with me."

An incredulous chuckle fell from his mouth. "Are you serious?"

I only stared at him.

"Bridges . . . Ray . . . no. She's not here. What . . . what are you thinking, man? Are you high? You been doing drugs? I've always kind of pegged you as a druggie."

"You're him," I said confidently. "You're the Hacketstown Hacker."

Now he only stared at me, his jaw slack. His stare was soft. I felt examined, as if he were trying to assess if I was sincere or not. I gave up nothing.

"Ray . . . no. I'm not the Hacketstown Hacker."

"But your certificates? The diplomas on the wall? The medical school stuff, the Hacketstown Hacker is most likely a rusty surgeon. Someone out of practice. Someone with training who hasn't done it in a while." My hand rose from the floor, and I extended one finger in his direction. "You."

He smiled. "No. Ray, no. I'm not . . . this is so ridiculous I don't even know what to say or where to begin."

"Just tell me the truth. You have the upper hand here, Glen. You can kill me after you tell me the truth. I just . . . I just want to hear it."

He looked at his shotgun, which was now pointed more toward the floor. Then he glanced back at me. "I'm not the killer, Bridges."

"The Hacketstown Hacker hasn't killed anyone. He's been—"

"I know what he's been doing," he said, cutting me off. "I've seen it on the news. Now listen to me, and listen to me good. I am not the Hacketstown Hacker. I am not abducting women and I am not hacking off their limbs." He shook his head at me. "What the hell has gotten into you, Bridges? If it's drugs, I can help you. Help you by getting you help."

I didn't believe him, but then he dropped the barrel of the shotgun on the floor, holding it like a walking crutch.

"Fine then. I'd like for you to get the hell out of my home." He waved me up off the floor. "Come on."

I stood up. "Prove it first."

"Prove it?"

I nodded. "Let me search your house. I've already been in the basement . . . it's clean."

"No shit." He let loose an exasperated sigh and hung his head to the side. "Then will you leave?"

I put my hands up. "Quickly and quietly."

He stepped aside. "You have five minutes."

Five minutes later, I was standing on Glen's porch, facing the street. The front door slammed closed behind me, rattling the snow-white winter wreath.

Glen's house had been clean. His attic, too. There were no women in there, no evidence anyone had been hacked to bits. No tools out in the open, none hiding in the closets. I only had five minutes, but I feel I conducted a pretty thorough search. And I might have gone a minute over, but Glen had been gracious enough to let me continue. Ease my mind. Search everything and everywhere.

He was clean.

He wasn't the Hacketstown Hacker.

Kayla *was still missing.*

I began my hike back to the main drag, getting out my cell phone and thumbing through my apps. As I clicked on the Uber icon, a car turned down the street, the headlights nearly blinding me. I watched as it slowed down after spotting me. I thought it would roll on by while maintaining its speed, but no—it kept slowing down.

Then it stopped right beside me. I recognized the car. The driver rolled down the window.

"Tough night?" the driver asked.

"You could say that."

Mark Barr, the store manager who hardly ever came into the store, smiled at me. "What are you doing out here so late?"

"I was . . . uh . . . at a friend's house."

He nodded, still smiling. "Can I give you a lift?"

"That's okay. I was just about to call an Uber."

He waved away the nonsense. "Get in. I'll drive you."

I debated it. Then decided a free ride could mean a little financial cushion this week. He opened the door and I ducked inside.

"Thanks, Mark. I appreciate this."

"Think nothing of it."

"So what are you doing out this late?"

He laughed. "Oh, you know. I like to enjoy the nightlife once in a while."

I forgot he wasn't married. "True. Well, this is the wrong town for that."

"Oh, this town is great. You just gotta know where to look."

"You live around here?"

"Two blocks down."

"Damn. I'd hate for you to drive all the way over to my place."

He took the car out of park, began driving. "We could stop at mi casa first? Just for a few beers, my treat. I picked up some cans from that new brewery that opened in town. I know it's late, but what the heck. You're not scheduled to open, are you?"

"Nope."

"Good. I won't take *no* for an answer then." He lightly punched my arm like we were the world's best buddies. "It'll be good to get to know you a little better."

"All right," I said.

I was tired. Drained. In desperate need of sleep. In desperate need of finding Kayla. I knew I shouldn't have taken the ride with Mark.

But life, sometimes, has a funny way of making rights out of wrongs.

TWENTY-SIX

I planted myself on Mark's couch and looked around the room, taking in the bachelor's living room décor. Or lack of. It was pretty plain, bare, not much in the way of the home furnishing. It lacked charm, and I gained the sense he wasn't much of a homebody.

A few seconds later, he set a glass of something dark amber in front of me, the inch of foam bubbling just above the rim.

Mark took a sip from his own glass, then licked his lips, savoring the delicious, bitter taste. "It's an amber ale. Pretty tasty. Enjoy."

I did enjoy. Half the beer was gone in about five minutes.

"Whoa, buddy," he said, reclining in his chair. "Don't drink it too fast. Might go to your head."

"Doesn't taste like there's a lot of alcohol in it."

"Don't let it fool you." He smiled. A warm smile. A welcoming smile. A smile that said 'You're safe here, Bridges. You're safe here.'

He kicked his feet up on the Ottoman.

"So, Bridges. You've been at Best Tronics for . . . what? Three years now?"

"Yeah," I said, looking down into the dark drink. All I saw

there was Kayla, drowning beneath the surface. Her, kicking her legs, screaming out for someone to come and save her. Some invisible force dragging her beneath the thinning layer of foam. Down into the amber ocean, dark depths from which she would never return. "Yeah, three years."

"You ever think about . . . saaaaay, a promotion?"

I had considered it. My life wasn't going anywhere else. Why not make the best of a decent situation? "Yeah, sometimes."

"Cool." Another swig of beer. His tongue navigated the interior wall of his cheeks. "Very cool. I'll let Glen know. We have a few positions opening up–receiving manager, for one–and I'll tell him I recommend you. Highly."

"Aren't you the store manager? Don't you make the decision all on your own?" Normally I wouldn't ask such a thing, in fear I'd come off sounding like an asshole, but he was right, the beer was starting to go to my head. Directly. With no filter. Even the room began to swerve a bit, which was odd considering I had only imbibed half the glass's contents. I needed to take it slow. Enjoy myself.

Kayla. Find her.

He laughed my comments off, though. A good laugh. A hearty laugh. A laugh that said 'You're too funny, Bridges', a laugh that told me he didn't think of me as an asshole. "Yes, yes, I *could.* But I don't want to be that kind of manager. I like to let my people make decisions. I like to be a behind-the-scenes guy. I'll be there when I'm needed, sure, and apply pressure if the situation calls for it, but ultimately, that's why I have a team. To execute on my behalf." More beer down his gullet. He was almost halfway done, too, showing no signs of slowing up. I had two inches at the bottom of my glass and it was going fast. "Also makes it easier to hold them accountable."

I nodded. I didn't know what the hell he was talking about. I kept seeing Kayla floating in the bottom of my glass. Drowned. Dead. Someone had put quarters over her eyes. They were shining like supernovas, bright and silvery, beautiful but dead.

"How are you feeling?" Mark asked. I blinked and his beer was gone. He was getting up for another one.

I quickly finished off mine. "Good. Real good."

"Ready for round two?"

"Absolutely."

I handed him the empty glass with Kayla's corpse inside of it.

An icky feeling stuck to my insides. My pores opened and streams of sweat spilled out. My pits grew swampy and moist, and I felt a cool, wet tickle run down my sides. The room began to tilt like an amusement park ride, one of those tilt-a-whirl kinds, only the motion was slow. I didn't feel ill, not exactly, but I could tell this was a prelude to me sticking my face in the toilet and unloading everything I'd eaten that day. And drank.

The beer.

The goddamn beer.

Mark returned a few seconds later, two glasses in hand, both filled to the brim. He stopped when he saw me.

"Oh my," he said, not overwhelmingly concerned. He set both beers down on the coffee table, on generic coasters. "Didn't expect it to hit you so quickly."

The world's smallest smirk lured his lips to one side.

I tried to stand up; found I couldn't. My legs weren't working. The muscles seemed to enter a state of atrophy. I was dead from the waist down.

"What . . ." I said, and found speaking a lot more difficult than it had been only moments ago. My face tingled with a numb sensation. Something insidious rested at the bottom of my stomach, anchoring me to the couch.

The beer.

If it was what he'd given me.

"Did. You. Give. Me?"

He smiled, his hands coming together like the jaws of a bear trap. "Just a little something to take the edge off. You're wound much too tight, Bridges."

My eyes darted around the room. Fuchsia, shades of purple and pink, filled the room. Gave everything a trippy vibe. The room still slid sideways, off its axis, floating, as if buoying on gentle ocean waters. At least I had that much control left. I wondered how long I had until I didn't. Until I was nothing but a sack of human flesh, my organs pilfered.

My limbs.

I had no idea what was happening to me.

"You know . . ." Mark said, kicking off his shoes, placing his bare feet back on the ottoman. He grabbed the beer he'd poured for himself, leaving mine to rest on the coaster. I didn't notice before, but now I saw the two were slightly different in terms of color. Mine was a shade darker than his. Just a tinge. Hardly noticeable unless you were looking. ". . . I've enjoyed watching you over the years. You've been an interesting subject."

"Subject." I barely recognized my own voice. It was drowsy and subdued, like my lips were too fat for the words to pass through.

"Yes. The second I told Glen to hire you, I knew you were special. It turned out, I was right."

"Right."

"Yes. See, I did an awful amount of research on you. Followed you places. Learned your likes and dislikes. Got real . . . ah, *intimate* with you."

I blurted out something. It was hardly coherent.

"Sounded like you asked *why? Why would you do such a thing?"* He chuckled. "It's simple really. I knew you were like me. That you seek desires outside the norm, what society tells us to like and dislike, what the media and advertising corporations direct us to enjoy and shun. I knew you had strange tastes just by looking at you, talking to you, spending five minutes alone with you in a professional setting. And like all good predators, Bridges, I can *smell my own."*

I wish I had the power to speak; I would have told him to fuck off, that I was nothing like him, nothing at all.

I was vaguely aware of where this was heading. What he was getting at. And I was forced to listen. On the couch, I could no longer move my arms. I had sat back, become one with the fabric. A permanent fixture in Mark's bland décor.

"I followed you to one of your meetings. It was during the first week you worked there. The two-hour drive was a bit much, don't you think?" No answer from me, of course. Mummified from the drug he'd slipped into my ale, I could only look on. Watch. Observe. Pray this would all end soon. "Well, I get it. You needed to protect yourself. After all, you were pretending to be a cripple, a man who'd lost his hand in a . . . what was it? A meat slicing accident?" He clicked his tongue against the roof of his mouth several times. "Very naughty of you to lie about such a thing. I wonder how you sleep at night." He laughed and waved his hand, the statement clearly facetious. "But once I found out the reason, I was . . . well, impressed for one. Also intrigued. You were acting on your desires, even though they were well outside of the norm. And I applaud you." He stood up and clapped like I'd just finished a one-man play and crushed it. Then he toured the living room, occasionally sipping from his glass. "I too act upon my desires," he said pensively. "Men, or women for that matter, shouldn't *not* act a certain way just because of what our society dictates. No, we as humans should live life the way it was meant to be lived. Free. Unrestrained. *Go without sin* is something that should be erased from bibles everywhere. There should be no laws, nothing tells us how to behave, how to treat one another. We were designed to live out how we see fit. We should exist how we damn well please."

Aggravation had bled into his voice, and the longer he spoke the more amped he became.

"We are animals, in reality. There's nothing that separates us from them. Chemically speaking, of course. We're all energy. We all occupy space. We all act on impulses, the very things wired into our head from the onset of our inception. The difference is, there are consequences for our actions. Rules we must abide by, so our modern society demands. Very unlike the animal world."

He closed his eyes and shook his entire body like a wet dog, as if the wetness were his anger and he was releasing it into the air. After that, a smile broke his face in half, one filled with sadistic intentions. He leaned forward, throwing his feet off the ottoman. Then he stood, marched over to the mantle above the fireplace. I hadn't noticed it before—or maybe I had, but it seemed to blend in well with the room somehow—but a giant sword rested there, encased in glass. He popped open the display case and removed the sword, the long metal blade gleaming even under the dimmed, fuchsia lighting. Slashing the air several times, he danced around the immediate area like he were Ninja-fucking-Gaiden. Even made *whooshing* sounds with his mouth as he cut into nothing.

"The sword is the ultimate weapon, don't you think? The sword has power. It's an intimate tool. Not like a gun. A gun is easy to use. There's distance between you and your target. There's no sense of closeness, no shared moment. No attachment to the violence. You become disconnected from the pain. But a sword . . ." He held the sword over his head and brought it down, aiming for between my legs.

I could only watch on in horror.

The blade cut through the air in slow motion.

I kissed the lower half of me goodbye.

Closed my eyes. Heard a loud thwack. Waited for the pain to settle in. That rush of fire that would burn through me with the rage of a thousand hells.

But none came.

I opened my eyes and saw the coffee table had been split in half. Our beers had fallen to the floor, spilled across the carpet, which didn't seem to bother Mark in the least. Something told me he'd spilled worse things than beer on the floor.

Blood.

Lakes of blood.

I tried to open my mouth, but my jaw was locked shut, no longer open for business.

Mark grinned at me, then went back to admiring his weapon. "Be right back," he said, and then he left me alone on the couch.

I stared at the wall and my eyes filled with tears the moment he left the room. I'd come to the realization these were going to be my last moments. I was going to die. A few years ago, I might have been okay with this. I'd been depressed, even tried to take my own life. Sometimes those thoughts still came, snuck up inside you when you were least expecting it, but lately I had been good. Without the aid from pills.

But now, I was anything but depressed. I was happy.

I wanted to live.

I wanted to love.

I wanted Kayla.

TWENTY-SEVEN

HE came back ten minutes later, rolling a hospital gurney into the room. On the stretcher, a woman lay fastened. She squirmed beneath her restraints, the nylon ratchet straps that held her there. Her mouth was stuffed with a black ball gag, yet she continued to yell and shout, plead for her release.

It wasn't Kayla, though. At first glance, I thought it had been her. Mark was probably keeping her in the house somewhere, maybe the basement, chained to the wall just like I'd pictured over at Glen's. The girl on the gurney, however, was one of the abducted women from the newspaper articles, one of the ones missing for the past week or so. I recognized her picture. She continued to thrash and the gurney clicked along with her movements, sounding as if the plastic and metal pieces holding the whole thing together would break if pressured enough. But the straps held her and so did the bed, and Mark didn't seem the least bit concerned with her feeble attempts to break free.

"I've envied you, Bridges, for quite some time." He held the sword like a walking stick, the tip digging into the carpet. "I've followed you. Lived vicariously through your midnight escapades. Hell, I've created *for* you. All these lovely little scenarios. Every cut, every amputation was all for you and the people like you. The people who think they're sick, who hide from society, who act in the shadows and aren't comfortable revealing themselves in fear that they'll be ridiculed and tormented, or worse, cast out from society, forever locked inside a lonely, miserable existence." That damn smile broadened. "I've created for *you*, Bridges."

My eyes bulged with confusion.

"Yes," he said, chuckling. "In a way, I guess you could call me your very own personal Dr. Frankenstein. I've created these monsters, and all so you could reap the reward. So you could go out and indulge in your darkest fantasies, live life the way it ought to be lived . . . like an animal."

They're not monsters, I wanted to tell him. *They're beautiful. And I'm no goddamn animal.*

"I am their god. And you have benefitted from my creations. How many of my *girls* have you taken to bed?"

I thought of Wendy, the look on her face when she'd told me the truth about her arm.

"I bet the number is much higher than you can imagine. I've been busy over the last three years. And you've been very busy, Bridges. Very busy indeed."

I winced.

The girl on the gurney bucked, rocking her ride back and forth, not hard enough to tip over, if that was her intention.

Mark put a hand on her chest. "I'm going to create again. Tonight. Her name is Annabelle and she's twenty-four years old. Isn't she pretty?" He threw his head back and laughed like any good arch nemesis. "I know she's not your type—yet—but we can fix that. One smooth cut. You know, Glen actually taught me a few things about incisions and keeping wounds clean and how to sew up an amputation to perfection. YouTube showed me what he and his books couldn't. I was pretty bad in the beginning, not confident, and lacking the experience needed to pull this off. But practice makes perfect, doesn't it? Yes, it does, and I've become pretty good at it. Even the papers compliment my work, say it's 'borderline professional', which I have to say, is great for the ego."

I breathed out a word that sounded a lot like *monster.*

This only made him snicker. "A monster? Me?" He shrugged nonchalantly. "Maybe. Gods can be monsters, I guess. But then again, aren't we all created in God's image? If so, then we're monsters too. Guilty by association," he said with a singsong voice.

I tried to shake my head. Don't know how it appeared, but he didn't seem to notice.

"Enough talk. Time to make you a new girl, Bridges. This one will be very nice. Should I take the left arm or the right arm? Do you have a preference?" He pointed at her thigh with the tip of the blade. "I'll even take off a leg, if it pleases you more. A little more work on my end, a lot more meat to slice, but it'll be worth it for both of us."

A noise stayed in my throat, low and guttural. I trembled uncontrollably, and not because the bastard had the heat cranked down, almost off. It *felt* like an OR in here.

"What's that? Oh, you want to know where Kayla is?" He flashed a grin that displayed every single one of his perfect teeth. "Don't worry, Bridges. She's next. Saving the best for last. We're gonna have a lot of fun with her." He lowered the sword to the girl's right shoulder. "So . . . right arm it is."

He brought the sword up over his head. The girl screamed with everything she had. The outburst barely made it past the gag, but I heard it with clarity, even in my drowsy state. Her eyes popped from her skull. Mascara streamed down her face as an endless train of tears kept rolling.

The sword came forward, cutting through the air. A blur flashed, bright and shiny in the magenta-haze of the living room. Next came the sound of something hard hitting meat, and sticking there, embedded in the dense mass.

The arm didn't come off completely on the first try. It hung by a few threads, red, stringy strands that looked like bloody rubber bands.

The girl screamed, hollering out for someone to come save her, though all the room heard was inarticulate noise. Her eyes drifted over to her ruined shoulder, and then she passed out.

Blood soaked the carpet.

I closed my eyes.

"Goddammit," Mark said. "I hate it when they pass out. Ruins the moment, you know?"

I listened to the sword slash through the air again, and sever whatever was keeping the arm attached. A wet hollow sound of the limb hitting the blood-drenched carpet was injected into my brain, a sound I'd never forget no matter how long I lived.

"There we go," Mark said proudly.

I didn't want to, but I found myself opening my eyes. Staring where the girl's arm used to be, which—now—was only a red cavity that leaked like an ineffective sprinkler. It dribbled onto the carpet freely, no signs of letting up.

I retched in my mouth, felt the acidy taste burn up the back of my throat. Involuntary, I swallowed. I wasn't sure if I was starting to gain back some feeling or if my body's reflexes had acted out naturally. I didn't feel different. Still felt frozen, hollow, a shell of a human being. Everything inside of me had felt scooped out. Especially from the neck up.

Mark quickly attended to the wound, putting gauze pads on it, dumping antiseptic all over the girl's shoulder. It fizzled and foamed. He patted it until it was dry enough to stitch up.

I watched with morbid fascination as he closed the wound, stretching smile never leaving his face for a goddamn second.

I must've passed out during the surgery because I opened my eyes to Mark slapping my cheek. "Hey, wake up, Bridges. Wake up. Don't fall asleep on me. Not now. Not when I have so many gorgeous things to show you."

The room was brighter but blurrier; my vision slid sideways, buoying as if my scope of the world sat on a series of great waves. I squinted against the rush of light, and after about forty-five seconds, when my eyes had finally adjusted, I could see I was in a different room altogether. The gurney holding the armless girl was gone. The walls here were white and so was the floor, tiled with brilliant marble. There was no more weird purplish-pink shroud over the room. There was only white. There was a fireplace across from me, about fifteen paces away. A bearskin carpet was the only décor. Well, there was more, but I didn't see it yet on account of my eyes' inability to fully focus on anything near the ceiling, close to the light. I took notice of the lack of furniture, not a single piece in the entire room.

"Welcome to my trophy room," he said, and that was when I

saw it.

The décor.

I looked up and saw limbs fastened to the walls, all of them preserved in impeccable condition. Arms and legs, some of them fixed to plaques, some of them sitting in glass cases, all of them displayed on the white walls like a big-game hunter's proud display of animal heads.

I began to move.

Mark spoke from behind me, "Lovely, isn't it?"

I realized I was in a wheelchair, still unable to control my muscles, no signs of the feeling coming back anytime soon. Mark pushed me around the room, giving me the tour of his prized collection. My focus had come back enough to make out the names of the victims etched in stone underneath every single proud display. Jesus Christ, he even recorded the dates of when he rendered them an amputee, along with the town he'd taken them from. It was all there, every single detail. A detective's wet dream. There was enough evidence in the trophy room to have him locked up for a good long time. Forever, probably. Until he croaked of old age or until some gang member shanked him in his sleep. Fuck, I prayed for the latter, only I wished he could be awake when the knife went into his neck, ripping through the muscle and vital arteries, spilling his life out before him. Fuck, I prayed I could be there to see it, too. I wanted to watch him suffer, wanted to see him die.

Mark chuckled from behind me. "Gorgeous, isn't it? My collection. My *limbs*." There had to be two dozen appendages on display. He'd been right; he'd been at this thing for a while. Maybe even before I ever came to work at Best Tronics. Even though his work had gone on for years, the limbs looked as if they'd been taken yesterday. I was impressed with his taxidermy skills, even though thinking about it and the process and how he'd come to accomplish all of this made me want to fucking puke.

He rolled me over to a particular arm.

I read the name: *Wendy Adams.*

My gaze lowered to the floor in shame.

"You remember her, don't you?"

I didn't answer. Obviously I couldn't, but if I had been able to speak, I'm not sure I would have anyway.

"I almost gave this one to you as a gift instead of the fresh one, but I thought you'd value the raw nature over sentimentalism. You can still have this one if you want. I'll happily take it down for you. Box it up." He knelt in front of me. "Blink twice if you'd like to have it."

In defiance, I kept my eyes open as long as I could. Then I clenched them shut when they started to water. At least I still had that much control over myself. I could move my eyelids.

It was a start.

Another smug laugh escaped his mouth. "You should embrace this. Stop fighting it." He waved a limp wrist at me. "You'll come around soon. In fact, I think you'll come around when you see your one true love . . . *Kayla.*"

The very mention of her name, the sound of it coming from his mouth, made me go wild. Until that moment, I didn't realize I had more control over my body than I previously thought. But as soon as the name left his mouth, I was moving, thrashing, flailing in the wheelchair. Of course, the drug was still running strong and my movements were restricted, but it was enough to cause Mark to leap back.

"Whoa! Easy there, tiger. Guess that stuff is starting to wear off. Don't worry, I have plenty where that came from." He removed a small vial from his lab coat's front pocket. It was a little less than half empty, but the single swig would be enough to keep me incapacitated for the next hour, at least. Possibly longer. He opened the vial, tilted my head back, and poured the liquid down my throat, shaking out every last drop. Then he closed my mouth, pinched shut my nose, and forced me to swallow. I had no choice, unless I never wanted to breathe again. It tasted like the strongest alcohol I'd ever tasted, and it burned all the way down into my stomach. It started working immediately, and the room began to fuzz out like an old television set.

"Now then," he said, wheeling me toward the door. "Shall we move on to tonight's main event?"

Back in the living room, he led Kayla before me, parading her around like a dog on a leash. She'd been dressed in a white hospital gown and that was it. He'd placed a collar around her neck and dragged her into the room with a long chain, the clink of metal sounding off like thunder in the relatively quiet moment. There was an empty medical bed in the corner, standing upright, waiting for another customer. Waiting for Kayla. She was crying, her face glistening with fresh tears. The wet emotional response, fear and sadness, poured more steadily the second she saw me.

"Ah, what a lovely reunion. Not the way you imagined it though, huh, Bridges? Bet you thought it'd be all butterflies and rainbows and rides on magical unicorns across endless fields of green expanse. Something pure and perfect, something you'd find in the greatest fairy tales ever written."

My mouth was numb, as was the rest of my body. I couldn't respond, forced to subscribe to this madness, whatever Mark had in store for the rest of the night.

His grin twitched. "I hate to deny you those treasured moments, I really do. But one day, in the future, you'll look back on this day and thank me. You'll thank me for doing what you'd never have the stones to do: make your one true love the way your heart desires. To make her agreeable to the monster inside you."

I am not a monster, I kept telling myself. Repeatedly, I heard the words, over and over, a never-ending mantra. I wanted to close my eyes but I'd lost control of that too. I felt something tickle the skin under my eyes and, after a delayed realization, I knew I was crying too. This only made Kayla cry harder, her body heaving along with her heavy sobs.

"Aw," Mark said, pouting his lower lip. "This doesn't have to be the sad moment you're making it out to be, my little friends." That goddamned smile returned, that ear-to-ear split across his face. Every one of my nightmares from here on out–if I lived to dream again–would contain that grin. "This should be a celebratory moment in both your lives. I am uniting two lovers, two souls that were meant to be together. Right? You feel that, that electricity in the air, that special charge, that current taking the room by storm?" He sniffed the air like a wolf catching the scent of something savory. "It's alive, your love. I can feel the thrum of its heartbeat inside me."

Kayla shuddered.

"Now, now," he said, running his knuckles along her cheek.

"Don't fret, little lamb. It'll all be over soon. I'll take a leg or an arm, and I'll have you stitched up in no time. You won't even know what's happened until it's over. Until you've been . . . *re-formed.*"

She shook her head, her body continuing to vibrate with absolute horror. The realization this was going to happen, there was nothing she or anyone else could do to stop it, finally settled in and she broke down, falling to her knees and trembling like an old engine on the verge of extinction.

He picked her up by her hair, forcing her back onto her feet. Her knees wobbled, barely able to support her weight. It didn't matter. He walked her over to the table and strapped her in. She offered no resistance. She'd succumbed to her fate. To whatever Mark had in store for her.

A collection of surgical tools sat on the table before her. Something that looked like a compact scythe caught my attention and I immediately imagined him using it on Kayla, running the blade vertically down her shoulder, taking the arm off in one swipe. The jet stream of blood that would surely follow.

My stomach tumbled over and over again.

Once Kayla was secured, he padded over to behind the couch where he'd set up a small recording studio—a camera on a tripod fully equipped with a boom mic, something he may have gotten from the store. Once he verified everything was running fine, he clapped me on the shoulder. I barely felt the impact of his hand coming down, gripping my flesh and bone.

"It'll all be over soon, Bridges. It'll all be over and you'll thank me. You and your love can be free. There won't be any more secrets between you. The elephant in the room will be gone. Poof!" He snapped his fingers. "Just like that."

I wanted to tell him she'd never love me, not when I told her my secret. Not when she discovered it was my fault she ended up here; she was about to lose a goddamn arm because I was too much of a coward and couldn't tell her the truth about me, about myself, about my condition, about how I felt, about the acrotomophilia. All of this could have been avoided if only I had grown a pair and unburdened my secrets. Came clean. Been honest with her. Shared everything with her.

But I was a coward. A fucking selfish asshole, too afraid of what other people would think of me, especially when I knew, when I *goddamn knew* she wouldn't judge me as if I were some sort of freak. I knew she wouldn't and I held out on her anyway, and look where that got us. Here. In this room with a man who was clearly off his rocker, who was clearly bat-shit crazy; a man who'd done some pretty terrible things and showed no signs of remorse, no signs of slowing down.

The Hacketstown Hacker.

Mark picked up the scythe. "What do you think?" He held up the instrument of destruction as if it were something worthy of a closer look. He seemed to like the way the light reflected off the shiny metal. "Too much?"

Obviously he got no comment from me.

"Nah, I think it'll do just fine."

Then he turned. Faced Kayla. Watched as any last shred of hope bled away from her features. Watched her tense, prepare for the inevitable damage coming. The swing of the scythe, the moment when her arm left her body, fell to the floor. The spurt of blood that would geyser from the fresh, crimson cavity.

Mark's feet shuffled forward, crinkling the plastic tarp beneath him.

He brought the scythe above his head. Held it there. Smiled. Then slashed down.

There was a scream.

And then, all hell broke loose.

TWENTY-EIGHT

THE next moment took place in a blink. I didn't see the shadow enter the room from the foyer; it flashed across the room in a streak, lightning quick. At first, my drug-addled mind told me an apparition had come to save us, a dark angel of goodwill. But even after that notion nestled in, I knew I was wrong, my senses were failing me. There was no such thing as angels, no such thing at all.

Anyway, here's what happened: A shadowy figure blurred across the room, barreling into Mark the second he began to bring the scythe down. The impact of the two bodies colliding was enough to knock Mark off his feet, even though Mark was bigger, built like a horse, and physically overmatched our savior in every possible way; the momentum and the quiet approach, the element of surprise, was enough to gain the upper hand. Mark was swept into the air and thrown backward, into the wall, near the window. His shoulder knocked into the glass, breaking the window. A glass shard punched into his arm, near the shoulder; the very same spot he'd aimed the scythe on Kayla. Blood blossomed on his shirt, the wound beneath opening wide, the flesh splitting like a squished banana peel.

Mark didn't take long to recover. Before our mystery guest

could decide what to do next, the boss had scrambled to his feet. He didn't even stop to survey his arm. His eyes fixed on his newfound enemy.

Then, he smiled. "Well, well. If it isn't another one of my good employees. How lovely to see you . . ." Mark's eyes were wide, feral. He was snarling and smiling all at once, which sounds impossible and contradictory, but his lips were literally curled in a way that resembled both actions.

Percy backed away from him, as if the man's rage were a force that drove him on his heels.

"Percy, Percy, Percy," he said, limping forward. My eyes found the source of his awkward gait. It appeared the tip of the scythe had pierced his right quad when he'd fallen against the wall. Dark red dripped steadily from the half-dollar-sized hole. Droplets fell and stained the beige carpet as he plodded forward. "I've never killed someone before, but I think you've just made a case to be my first victim."

Percy squeaked and searched the immediate area for a weapon. He nearly tripped over the stone slab in front of the fireplace. Next to the fireplace was the katana Mark had used to clip the other girl's arm. It was still heavily coated with her blood, not quite dry. Sticky and lumpy, but still a healthy, bright scarlet streak.

He grabbed the sword before Mark could close the distance.

Blindly, he swung in Mark's direction. The sword cut through the air, making an audible *vroom* sound, like a homerun hitter swinging for the fences and missing the stitched leather by a country mile. Mark needed to do little to dodge the strike.

"You're a dead man, Percy Jones," he said through his teeth, reaching back with the scythe and ready to unload his fury.

He heaved the blade at Percy's head, and Percy ducked.

In one fluid moment, Percy jabbed the blade forward. Mark's momentum carried him into the tip. The sword's pointed end disappeared inside of Mark, at least six inches of metal sinking into the softest part of his belly below the ribcage.

Mark's eyes widened with surprise. His mouth opened, jaw unhinged, and his lips—no longer sporting that goddamn smile—took the shape of a giant O. A small, inward-breathing noise escaped his mouth, and the three of us each got the sense it was one of the last noises the man would ever make.

He dropped to his knees.

Percy helped him along by shoving the sword deeper. The blade pitched a tent on his back. An obscene amount of blood soaked the fabric. Red stains materialized from where the sword ran through all the way down his back, down his pant legs. He was bleeding way too much. There was no stopping it. And hell . . . not a single one of us wanted to.

Percy backed up. Mark tried to remove the sword from his abdomen, but it was a feeble, useless attempt. Like one of the townspeople trying to pull the sword free in *The Sword in the Stone*. It had been embedded, and would require a lot more strength than whatever Mark had left in his tank.

He opened his mouth. No words. Only sounds. Loose and garbled. Labored, wheezing breaths. He didn't make eye contact with anyone in the room. He was alone now. He'd die alone. The way he probably wanted.

He laid himself on the floor, curling into the fetal position. With no more desire to stave off the inevitable, he closed his eyes.

And died.

Even though Percy had won, there was no celebratory dance. No celebration of any kind. Not even a wisecrack, which mildly disappointed me, but Percy had just taken another man's life and I couldn't even imagine what that does to one's psyche. He stood there for minutes after Mark had taken his final sleep, just looking down at the body, the giant red puddle beneath it. Staring. Lost in what he'd done. Coming to terms that he was now a killer, wishing it could have ended differently. I got the sense even though onscreen blood and gore was his hobby, the phoniness of filmmaking had not desensitized him, or prepared him, for the real thing. The true horror of watching another person bleed out between your feet.

He turned and stumbled to his knees, making it to the fireplace before a stream of vomit spouted from his mouth. He puked several times before finding the strength to stand again. Once he was finished, he turned to us, realized we were both unable to move for very different reasons, and then proceeded to free us. He went over to Kayla first, unbinding the straps that tied her to the upright bed. Once free, she collapsed into his arms. I couldn't tell if she was pressing all her body weight on him in the form of a hug, or she didn't have the strength to stand on her own. Either way, he helped her over to the couch and sat her down.

Then he looked to me.

"You okay?" he asked.

I still couldn't respond. I tried to move my lips and was able to, but not enough to talk. My tongue was just as sluggish. I was able to grumble something, which I think meant, "I'm drugged."

"Did he drug you?" Percy asked.

I moved slightly.

He understood. "Holy fuck, man. This is crazy. I never should have left you."

But in the end, I was glad he did. If he hadn't, then he would have been on the couch with me, accepting Mark's tainted craft beer. He'd have been drugged and right beside me now, frozen, watching the horrors unfold. He would have seen that girl's arm get lopped right the fuck off. And Kayla . . . *God, Kayla.*

I snuck a glance at her. She stared at the carpet, a portion that wasn't soiled with Mark's blood. Catatonic. Mentally destroyed. Traumatized beyond her wits. I wondered how long it would take to repair the damage done here tonight.

"After I dropped you off," Percy said, "I went home. Laid in bed for like an hour. Couldn't sleep. Kept thinking you were in trouble." He shrugged, as if this were part of the story he couldn't aptly explain. "So I went back out. Headed back to Glen's. I was about to turn down his street when I saw you, talking to Mark. So I followed you. Back here."

I wanted to thank him. Throw my arms around him. Hug him. Tell him he was my new personal Jesus.

My lips were beginning to burn, tingle like Novocaine losing its effect. It was the greatest feeling in the world.

"I don't know why," he continued, "but I felt like you were in trouble. Even though I knew it was Mark, something seemed off about the whole thing. Him showing up like that. I secretly followed you here and . . . and I knew."

Knew what, Percy? What did you know?

"I knew Mark was the Hacketstown Hacker the second you went inside. I just knew it. Then . . . then I saw . . . through the window . . . I saw him take that girl's . . ." He whimpered softly, a mouse squeaking over a piece of cheese.

He did see. *Saw* what I'd seen. Saw Mark take that poor girl's arm clean off. Well, not clean. But . . . you know.

He sniffled. "I tried to find a way in. Once he took you away and cleaned up, I waited. Called the cops."

Where are they? Where are the fucking cops?

"They thought I was you. Calling in another false call. Said they already investigated one phony accusation tonight and they weren't sending any more officers out unless I had some proof. Can you fucking believe that? Fucking pigs, man." He shook his head. "Fuck. Anyway. I knew I had to act. By the time I got my shit together, worked up a plan, he was back in the living room. Kayla was tied up. You were on the couch, drugged I'd guessed. He was about to . . . *hack.*"

Percy dry-heaved. His throat gurgled.

He closed his eyes, trying to erase the images that lived there now.

"I had to do something," he said as if he had something in his mouth, a liquid. "So I just rushed in and . . . well, you know the rest."

"Thrk oo," I said, not realizing I had done so. Not at first.

"Shit, man. You're getting your feeling back."

A tingling sensation ran down the length of my arms and legs, my nerves swimming back to life. Kayla continued to sit there, brain-dead, staring. I felt for her. I couldn't wait to wrap my arms around her. Comfort her. Give her the reassurance that everything would be okay.

I dreaded apologizing to her, admitting everything was my fault. I feared telling her the truth because of what it could mean for our future. But I had to.

Goddammit, I needed to.

An hour later, the cops and ambulances arrived. It took half that long to convince them we weren't fucking around, we'd been victims and survivors of the Hacketstown Hacker, the last ones because the motherfucker was dead, rotting in a pool of his own demise.

On the ride to the hospital, I told Kayla everything.

Every single detail. My secrets. Everything I'd done. Every meeting I went to, every amputation I faked, every goddamn lie I told over the past ten years or so. My suicide attempt and brief mental breakdown when I was twenty-four that no one, not a single psychiatrist, could get to the bottom of—though, they didn't need to because I knew exactly why: *my head was full of secrets and lies and I couldn't hold them in all by myself.* It had happened once and I was sure it would happen again, which was why it felt good revealing the truth to Percy, and to a lesser degree, the shrink. Like I'd broken free from the anchor that tied me to these dark truths.

Anyway, I divulged every detail, told her everything, and ended with expressing how much I truly loved her, how much she meant to me, how I would do anything for her, and how I would walk through every circle of hell just to find a way to make *us* work.

She replied with three words: "I hate you."

And then she never spoke to me again.

TWO MONTHS LATER

WELL, she never spoke to me again *that* night. She ignored my texts during the three days she spent in the hospital. Her parents turned me away when I showed up at their house three days after that. Kayla didn't speak to me for two months. Two. Long. Fucking. Months.

Then, one day, out of the blue, with no absolutely no warning whatsoever, she showed up on my doorstep, arms folded across her chest and tears in her eyes.

"Can I come in?" she asked. The bruises on her cheeks, the cut above her eye, and her swollen lips had all healed.

I stepped aside and let her in.

The apartment wasn't in the cleanest state as I'd let some chores slip over the past two months following my brush with the Hacketstown Hacker. I had sunken into a minor, not-as-severe-as-the-last-time depression, and cleanliness had been the furthest thing from my mind. But I didn't care about the state of the place, the piles of clothes in the corner of each room, the two months' worth of mail stacked on the living room table. I was too surprised, too internally giddy to do anything about it.

She went for the couch.

I offered her a Coke.

"No, thank you. I won't be long."

That wasn't a good sign. When someone tells you they won't be long, it's often bad news. Least in my experience. That *let-me-say-my-final-piece* tone told me this was the end of everything. All the fun we'd shared, all the beautiful moments, the ups and downs, those rare, raw feelings, those exhilarating sensations in the pit of your stomach that go off like a bottle rocket in a butterfly house . . . well, this is where it all ended. It'd been a great ride, but this was where the love train pulled into the last station and let us off.

"I know what you're going to say," I said, plopping myself down in the loveseat across from her. "And you're right."

She couldn't even bring herself to look at me.

"I'm a monster," I said, and though it felt like a lie, it was probably the truest lie I'd ever told. "Everything that happened to you was my fault."

She covered her face with both hands and cried into them.

I wanted to comfort her. Put a hand on her shoulder. Squeeze her. Kiss the crown of her head. But I kept myself seated and waited for the sadness to let up.

"I can't begin to tell you how sorry I am, Kay."

She removed her hands and glared at me. "Why couldn't you be honest with me? I thought what we had was special?"

"It was." *It is,* I scolded myself. *It's still there. It's still* special. *Convince her.* "I mean, it *is* special, Kay. I've never felt about anyone the way I do you." I swallowed, waiting for her to come back at me, but she didn't. "That's why I lied. Hid the truth. I couldn't . . . shit, I couldn't have you think of me as some sort of . . . freak. A *monster.*"

"I wouldn't have."

I shrugged. "I know. I know. I fucked up."

"You nearly got me killed."

"I know. If there was a way to time travel, I'd fucking tell you everything the moment I met you." Squinting, I gave the idea a second thought. "I mean, maybe not everything. Not the moment I met you. I'd wait until the second date. It'd be too much of an info dump and you'd get all—"

"Ray," she said, cutting me off. "I get it."

I nodded. "Sorry."

She sighed, looking elsewhere in the room. Casting her eyes back on me, she chewed her bottom lip. "I don't hate you."

My heart danced. "Oh?"

"I'm sorry I said that to you in the ambulance. I was hurt. Mentally fatigued. I couldn't think straight. And then you were yammering at me, telling me all these . . . *things.* I didn't understand, not at the time."

"I tried reaching out . . ."

"I know. I just needed time. Time to myself. Time to heal. Not just from what happened at . . ." She froze, and for a moment, I thought I lost her to the memory of that night. ". . . not just from what he did to us, but for us to heal. You and me."

"I–"

She shook her head. "No, let me finish. You and me, Ray, we're like an open wound that keeps bleeding. You can cover it up, apply pressure, yet, it still *bleeds.* The only thing to do is stitch it up. Put closure to it."

I gulped down a ball of air. "So what're you suggesting?"

"We have two options: one, when I leave this apartment, we never see or speak to each other again. Time heals all wounds, and that's the truest shit I've ever heard. Eventually, we'll move on. Eventually, we won't think about each other. Eventually, a day will pass when we wake up and we're not the first thing we think of."

"And the other option?"

"We try to fix this little problem of ours."

I leaned back. "It's not something I can fix, Kay. It's a thing that's ingrained into my psyche. People with their limbs–"

"I'm not talking about your acrotomo-whateverthefuck."

Even her butchering the term made my stomach swim with nausea. I thought then that Mark Barr had cured me. Done what no doctor ever could. What no pill could fix. He'd taken my brain and rewired it with the simple act of maiming an innocent woman before my very eyes.

Tilting my head, I asked, "Then what?"

"Your lying."

Lightbulb. "Oh. Shit. Yeah, I'll never do that again. I will never, ever betray you like. You have my word. I swear on my life."

Her shoulders lifted. "How do I know you're not lying right now?"

"Believe me."

"How?"

"Trust me."

"But *how?*"

"I'll beg. You want me to beg?"

"It'd be a start."

"I'll get down on both knees."

"A proposal already? We're not quite there, Don Juan. I still haven't decided if I'm going to forgive you."

Something caught in my throat. A tear stung my eyes from their outside corners. A tug in my chest let me know this was real. Our story. Our love. All of it.

I dropped to both knees and took her hands. "Kayla, I swear to fucking God, whichever one you happen to believe in, and I don't know because we really haven't discussed it, but whichever one, I swear on them. I swear . . ."

She was weeping now. She gripped my hands hard; felt the pressure in my bones.

". . . I swear," I told her, feeling wetness trickle down the contour of my nose. "I swear on our . . . unborn children . . ."

Her eyes were waterfalls.

". . . that I'll never lie to you again. Never. Not once. No matter what. I will do nothing but love, respect, and honor you. Forever, and I fucking mean it."

She leaned in and kissed my lips, and I kissed back, and our lips were wet with tears and saliva and the prospect of our future.

The kiss went on for a long time, practically a new world record.

We left the apartment that afternoon holding hands.

I left knowing it'd all work out, it'd end like the perfect fairytale. We'd go through life, experiencing everything together, loving each other until we grew old and withered, until we became nothing but bone dust. We'd be able to fight anything and everything that came our way. Whatever sickness, disaster, or unordinary psycho-sexual condition stood in our way, we'd conquer the fucker.

Last year was the Winter of the Hacketstown Hacker.

This year was the Winter of Love. And just like last year, we came out on top. Alive and free. Changed, yet still the same. Better for it.

We lived. We loved. And goddammit . . . we loved well.

Acknowledgements

A huge shout-out to my wife, Ashley, who, without her support, none of this would be possible. Especially this book. While I can't say this story is based on true events, I can say it was "inspired" by true events, which may mean what you think it means, or it may not. I'll never say.

Anyway, also a huge "thank you" to Matt Hayward who encouraged me to keep writing this book when I didn't think I could. His input was invaluable.

ABOUT THE AUTHOR

Tim Meyer dwells in a dark cave near the Jersey Shore. He's an author, husband, father, podcast host, blogger, coffee connoisseur, beer enthusiast, and explorer of worlds. He writes horror, mysteries, science fiction, and thrillers, although he prefers to blur genres and let the stories fall where they may.

You can follow Tim at https://timmeyerwrites.com

Other Grindhouse Press Titles

#666__*Satanic Summer* by Andersen Prunty
#045__*As Seen On T.V.* by John Wayne Comunale
#044__*Where Stars Won't Shine* by Patrick Lacey
#043__*Kinfolk* by Matt Kurtz
#042__*Kill For Satan!* by Bryan Smith
#041__*Dead Stripper Storage* by Bryan Smith
#040__*Triple Axe* by Scott Cole
#039__*Scummer* by John Wayne Comunale
#038__*Cockblock* by C.V. Hunt
#037__*Irrationalia* by Andersen Prunty
#036__*Full Brutal* by Kristopher Triana
#035__*Office Mutant* by Pete Risley
#034__*Death Pacts and Left-Hand Paths* by John Wayne Comunale
#033__*Home Is Where the Horror Is* by C.V. Hunt
#032__*This Town Needs A Monster* by Andersen Prunty
#031__*The Fetishists* by A.S. Coomer
#030__*Ritualistic Human Sacrifice* by C.V. Hunt
#029__*The Atrocity Vendor* by Nick Cato
#028__*Burn Down the House and Everyone In It* by Zachary T. Owen
#027__*Misery and Death and Everything Depressing* by C.V. Hunt
#026__*Naked Friends* by Justin Grimbol
#025__*Ghost Chant* by Gina Ranalli
#024__*Hearers of the Constant Hum* by William Pauley III
#023__*Hell's Waiting Room* by C.V. Hunt
#022__*Creep House: Horror Stories* by Andersen Prunty

#021__*Other People's Shit* by C.V. Hunt
#020__*The Party Lords* by Justin Grimbol
#019__*Sociopaths In Love* by Andersen Prunty
#018__*The Last Porno Theater* by Nick Cato
#017__*Zombieville* by C.V. Hunt
#016__*Samurai Vs. Robo-Dick* by Steve Lowe
#015__*The Warm Glow of Happy Homes* by Andersen Prunty
#014__*How To Kill Yourself* by C.V. Hunt
#013__*Bury the Children in the Yard: Horror Stories* by Andersen Prunty
#012__*Return to Devil Town (Vampires in Devil Town Book Three)* by Wayne Hixon
#011__*Pray You Die Alone: Horror Stories* by Andersen Prunty
#010__*King of the Perverts* by Steve Lowe
#009__*Sunruined: Horror Stories* by Andersen Prunty
#008__*Bright Black Moon (Vampires in Devil Town Book Two)* by Wayne Hixon
#007__*Hi I'm a Social Disease: Horror Stories* by Andersen Prunty
#006__*A Life On Fire* by Chris Bowsman
#005__*The Sorrow King* by Andersen Prunty
#004__*The Brothers Crunk* by William Pauley III
#003__*The Horribles* by Nathaniel Lambert
#002__*Vampires in Devil Town* by Wayne Hixon
#001__*House of Fallen Trees* by Gina Ranalli
#000__*Morning is Dead* by Andersen Prunty

Printed in Great Britain
by Amazon

76623360R00106